Destined

••

Cheryl Morrison

Copyright © 2024 by Cheryl Morrison

All rights reserved.

No portion of this book may be reproduced in any form without written permission from the publisher or author, except as permitted by U.S. copyright law.

Contents

1. Chapter 1- Memory Lane — 1
2. Chapter 2- Meeting Mr. Taylor — 5
3. Chapter 3-Making New Friends — 10
4. Chapter 4- You Are Not My Dad — 13
5. Chapter 5- A Secret Revealed — 17
6. Chapter 6-Weekend with Jordan — 20
7. Chapter 7-What Did I Agree To? — 25
8. Chapter 8-Halloween — 30
9. Chapter 9- Rachel Was Always My Favorite — 35
10. Chapter 10-Torn Between Them — 40
11. Chapter 11- First Kiss — 46
12. Chapter 12- What Is This Girl Doing To Me? — 50
13. Chapter 13- Surprise Visit — 53
14. Chapter 14- I Know Who I Am Choosing — 58
15. Chapter 15- Mrs. Tarantino? — 63

16.	Chapter 16- Anthony AKA Seth	66
17.	Chapter 17- The Cat's Out Of The Bag	70
18.	Chapter 18- Best Night Of My Life	74
19.	Chapter 19- Crazy Ride Home	81
20.	Chapter 20- The Disappearance	85
21.	Chapter 21- Something Is Wrong	88
22.	Chapter 22- The Kidnapping	93
23.	Chapter 23- It's All Over Finally	98
24.	Chapter 24- Destined To Be Together	102
25.	Epilogue	106

Chapter 1- Memory Lane

Kendall (10 yrs old flashback)

I walk outside to feel the warm summer air kiss my skin as I set out on my daily adventure with my best friend. My best friend is my neighbor Seth. He's one year older than I am but we have so much fun together. We always find fun things to do together and he always makes me laugh. Not to mention he is also very cute, but I don't like him that way. I go to his house and his mom tells me he's outside already. I finally spot him in his back yard building some type of fort I assume for us to play in.

"Seth!" I yell excitedly as I get close enough for him to see me.

He turns and greets me excitedly.

"Kendall! Look what I built! It's a place for us to hang out this summer, what do you think?" He asks hopefully.

"I think it looks like fun. But what would be even more fun would be to have a water gun fight!!" I exclaim as I grab the hidden water gun I had tucked under my t shirt and began to fire a never ending shower of water right in his face as I laugh hysterically.

His look goes from happy to angry in a matter of seconds.

Oh crap I didn't think this through.

I turn around and run as fast as I can as Seth chases me around his yard all while I scream and laugh. He tackles me to the ground and steals my gun to do nothing other than assault me just as I did him. We laugh hysterically at each other for a while. We end up going on a bike ride, playing at the park with some of the other neighborhood kids and spending the rest of the day having probably the most fun I had ever had up until that point. It was one of the best days of my life.

The next day I wake up excitedly rushing over to Seth's house hoping to be able to repeat our previous day's adventures. I knock at the door but no one answers. No car is in the driveway. That's odd. Seth's mom and my mom both don't work and they always stay home with us in the summer time. Maybe they had to run an errand? I look inside to see the house is in shambles. Mrs. Tarantino wouldn't ever leave her house like this. She always kept her house very clean. Something is wrong. Mr. Tarantino is away on business a lot. He hasn't been home all week. I don't even know who mom and I can call to see if everything is ok?? I look around the back of the house and all of Seth's toys including his freshly built play house were all still there. Something has to be going on. This is just too weird. I run home to mom to tell her what I saw and to try and call Seth's mom on her cell phone. She does as I ask of her after seeing how frantic I was. After a few rings, Mrs. Tarantino answers the phone. My mom questions her and she says they would be back in a few weeks. That something was wrong with a family member and they had to go to see them suddenly. I calmed down when she told me that, knowing that all was ok and they would be back.

But they never came back. I lost my best friend and it took a long time to recover from it. We tried to contact them a few times after that but they just dodged our calls. The house eventually sold. I was devastated.

Kendall (Present Day-7 years later)

"Kendall?" My mom questions me breaking me from my memory.

"Yeah mom?" I ask her.

"You ok? You are awfully quiet." She persists.

"Yeah mom. Just tired." I lie.

I close my eyes faking like I am taking a nap so I don't have to talk. I listen to the hum of the tires hitting the pavement underneath our car as we travel down the highway. I am not sure what made me think back to my childhood just now. I think maybe I couldn't remember a time when I felt this lost and empty before. When Seth left that would be the only other time. This is worse though. So much worse.

My mom and I are driving down the interstate heading towards Chicago. I hated the city. I was a country girl and I liked my small town way of life. We are moving into the suburbs of Chicago and I was not happy about it at all. I will miss my little town of Redbud. I had to leave my friends, the only home I have ever known, and my sweet boyfriend Jordan. I am going to miss them so much. Jordan and I want to try to do the whole long distance thing but I don't think it's going to work. Long distance never works. I mean Chicago is 5 hours away from our former home.

I am being so negative I know. I just miss my dad and it hurts. He passed away about 8 months ago in a car accident. He was the only one of my parents that worked. My mom always stayed at home to take care of me and the house. But after he died, my mom was forced to get a job so we could afford to live. She sold our house to pay off all of my parents debts and packed us up to move. I was not happy about it at all. We fought, I screamed and cried and begged her not to leave. But what it came down to is that she would always be reminded of my father in my hometown. He was well liked and had a lot of friends. It was just a constant reminder of the pain from his sudden, unexpected death. She wanted a fresh start. Plus there were more job opportunities near the city and ways for her to make more money to support us. We weren't moving directly into the city but in the outskirts of it in a town called Arlington Heights. We are going to rent a townhouse for the time being until we get more financially stable. As mad as I was at mom at first about this move, I am trying to make the best of it. All we have left is each other and the loss of my father was so painful I couldn't sever my relationship with my mother.

We pull into the parking lot of our new town home. We get out and walk inside and I scope the place out. It's not too terrible actually. We each get our own bedroom and bathroom and the rooms are decently sized. I am going to try hard for my mother to make this place home. I always loved going on those adventures with Seth when we were little. I am just trying to treat this same situation as a new adventure.

Chapter 2- Meeting Mr. Taylor

Kendall POV

I wake up feeling pretty refreshed. I stretch out across my bed before getting up to shower. I had a long nights sleep after a tiring week. We spent the first week here unpacking our stuff and learning our way around the area. My mom met her new boss and coworkers and seems to be very happy.

After I shower and get ready my nerves start getting the better of me. Today is my first day at my new school and it's also my mom's first day at work. A buzz from my phone gets my attention.

Have a great first day. Miss you. -Jordan

My heart flutters in my chest. He is so sweet and caring. I type up a quick response.

Thank you. I am nervous but I am going to do my best to get through it. Miss you too.

I hit the send button and put my phone away in my bookbag. My mom and I wish each other a great first day as we both head out the door. My mom offers to drive me but I decide to walk to help ease some of my nerves. It's nice that the school is only a few blocks from my house.

I walk into the school and head to the front office to get my schedule. They greet me warmly and I am off to find my first class. I am walking the halls slowly and I get a series of dirty looks, wolf whistles, and snickers. Wow. Not a good start. I find my first class and walk inside and introduce myself to the teacher.

"Guys this is Kendall Thomas. She is new here. Please make her feel welcome." The teacher says in a semi monotone voice.

The class just stares back at me with looks of disgust and complete indifference. Wow this is going to be a great junior year I think to myself. I find an empty seat towards the back of the room. Two girls keep whispering and laughing and looking my way. Then I notice a very nerdy guy push his glasses down and raise his eyebrows my way as he checked me out.

Gross.

I sit in class trying to pay attention while the other kids goof off and talk. Is it always like this? After a very painful class period, the bell rings and I am back to searching for my next class. I am definitely not in my small town of Redbud anymore. If we would see new students we went out of our way to help them. Not one person has even offered to show me around or just be even the slightest bit nice to me. Gosh this is going to be the worst year ever I can just feel it.

I suddenly almost run into a couple making out heavily in the hallway. I immediately side step them but accidentally bump into someone hard in the process and almost fall backwards. Had the person not caught me I would have. I look up into the eyes of my savior and the familiarity hits me like an ice cold splash of water to my face. I see those familiar baby blue eyes that I remember staring back into so many years ago. I am rendered almost speechless until I finally manage to mutter out "Seth?" so low it's almost a whisper.

His eyes widen in surprise for a moment before his demeanor completely changes to a scowl and his eyebrows furrow.

"My name is Anthony Taylor." He scoffs. "I have never seen you before in my life. You must be confusing me for someone else." He says rudely.

He looks so much like Seth it's uncanny. He must have a twin out there. I know it's been 7 years but his face hasn't changed much other than the facial stubble that litters his cheeks. He of course got way taller and oh my God is he hot. He is extremely built and really nice to look at. He notices me check him out and he gives me a tiny, cocky smirk and as I realize he saw me looking at him, I blush and lower my gaze to the floor.

A voice makes me hold my head up suddenly, "Baby? Who is this?" A girl asks Anthony showing distaste towards me.

"She's no one. Let's go." He says as he grabs her arm and they walk quickly down the hallway.

Geez. So rude. Is everyone in this place like this??

After a long day of much of the same, I come home and soon after mom joins me.

"How was your first day?" She asks as she slumps down on to couch and puts her feet up immediately.

"It was.......interesting." I withhold my true feelings so I don't upset mom. She has enough going on. But I know she senses my frustration.

"Well honey, it will get better. People will get to know the wonderful person that you are and you will make lots of friends." She says encouragingly.

"Speaking of friends I ran into a long lost friend today or atleast he was his twin because he said his name was Anthony. But I swear he looked identical to Seth." I tell her.

"Really? That's crazy! You haven't seen him in like 7 years right? I am sure he has changed some. You haven't said his name in so long. It takes me back to your childhood." She says reminiscingly.

"How was your day mom?" I ask changing the subject. I can tell she was thinking of dad. I can always tell.

"Well it was ok. It's going to be an adjustment. I have a lot to learn, but the people I work with are all very welcoming." She tells me smiling.

Boy I wish I could say the same. I think to myself.

I need to just become an adult already. Teenage drama sucks.

"Are you ready to eat?" My mom asks breaking me from my thoughts.

I nod my head and we eat dinner continuing to talk about our days trying to focus on the positive and not the negative. Although I can't think of much positive at the moment. I miss Jordan and I need to talk to him.

I head to my bedroom and FaceTime Jordan. He answers almost instantly.

"Hey!! I miss you so much!" I beam happily when I see his face.

"Hey beautiful! I miss you too. I can't wait to come visit you in a few weeks. This is so hard but I want to make this work." He tells me sincerely.

"I can't wait until I see you either. I am trying to adjust to my new school but I just don't know. The people here just aren't as friendly." I tell him honestly.

"Babe, you will make friends. Just keep being you and someone will soon see how awesome you are." He tells me sweetly.

He always knows how to make me feel better.

"Well I have to go to bed, I will talk to you tomorrow." I tell him.

"Night." He tells me as I say the same thing in return and we hang up.

I lay in bed tossing and turning that night thinking of all the scenarios in my head of what is going to happen tomorrow at school. It has to be a better day. I am going to make it one. I think to myself before I doze off.

Chapter 3-Making New Friends

Kendall's POV

I walk into school with a more confident attitude. I decided that I am not going to listen to the rude comments from other students and hopefully I will find someone that is friendly towards me. That's all I care about right now other than focusing on school work.

My first class period is much like it was yesterday but my second period was better. We had to partner up with people and just when I thought I would never find someone to work with me and that I would be doing this activity alone, a girl speaks up that I hadn't noticed before and says she will be my partner. I smile at her and she smiles back. Finally someone that is nice for a change. We make our way over to each other and begin our introduction.

"I know you are new here but I never got your name?" She questions.

"Oh! My name is Kendall! What's yours?" I say in return.

"My name is Julie." She replies. After our intros, we start to get busy on our activity.

Class flew by quickly and soon enough the bell was ringing for lunch. Julie asked me if I wanted to sit with her and another friend at lunch and I was ecstatic. I said yes probably a bit too eagerly.

"Sarah, this is Kendall. She's new here and I invited her to eat lunch with us." Julie says as she introduces me.

"Hi Kendall. Where did you move from?" She questions.

I spend the whole lunch telling them all about myself and also asking questions about them. They are both very sweet and I am so thrilled to finally have friends.

The rest of the day goes by quickly and uneventfully, but just as the bell rings for dismissal I get up excitedly to go home to tell my mom all about my friendships I made, and that's when a girl trips me and I fall flat on my face. My nose and lip are bloodied and I am absolutely mortified. I look up through teary eyes to look at my assailant, hoping this was all just an accident but what she says confirms it was just the opposite.

"Watch where you are going bitch!!" She yells in my face before throwing my things at me and walking away laughing with her friends.

Well I almost had a great day. I get up and head to the bathroom to clean myself up. After finishing, I am finally able to leave to head home when I notice Anthony is staring at me from across the school yard. It felt like his gaze was looking through my soul. It was intense. As I got a little closer to him his face changed. Was that pity that I saw? Probably because my face looks awful. His face then turns back to a scowl and he turns to walk away. That was weird.

After I make it home I text my new friends to tell them what happened. So glad we exchanged numbers. They told me that all was going to be ok and the hype that surrounds being a new kid will wear off eventually and I will mesh right in with everyone else. Boy I hope that is sooner rather than later. Not sure how much longer I can deal with all the negative attention.

The next day was a little less eventful. Other than some guy spilling his drink all over my shirt. I had to borrow a shirt from Sarah and although it was tighter and lower cut than I was used to wearing I was thankful to have something else to wear.

As I was walking down the hall towards my next class I saw Anthony from down the hallway. His eyes locked on me again. He didn't break eye contact until someone started talking to him. He smiled at them and that was the first time I had seen him smile since I had been here. I would pay money to see him smile like that at me. Wait. What am I saying? He's cocky and rude. But something draws me to him. Like a magnetic force. Maybe it's the fact that he reminds me so much of Seth? I am not sure. But something tells me there is a strange connection between us. I mean could he really be Seth? Would he lie to me? I think I am officially losing it.

Chapter 4- You Are Not My Dad

Kendall's POV

I decide that after having so many stare downs with Anthony that I am going to ask Julie and Sarah about him out of curiosity. I don't want it to sound like I am digging for info too much but I need some answers. We sit down to lunch and I begin my quest for knowledge.

"So what do you guys know about Anthony Taylor?" I begin my questioning.

"You mean the most popular guy in school that is a senior and totally gorgeous? Yeah we know him." Sarah answers as she and Julie both giggle.

"Why are you asking?" Julie questions me.

"Well every time I am in the hallway I see him staring at me. At first I thought it was all in my head but it's weird. It's like I can feel it when he does it." I explain.

"Oh well I wouldn't look too much into it. He may just be trying to read you since you are new in town. He has a girlfriend, Cassie Johnson. She's the most popular girl in school. They are the couple that rules the school. She is the head cheerleader and he is the lead pitcher for our baseball team. They have gone to states every year since he started here." She explains.

I give her a questioning look so she continues without me even having to ask.

"He moved here in 10th grade. He instantly fit right in. I mean when you look like that it makes sense. He has moved around a lot. Apparently his dad is in the military. I think he is looking forward to graduation so he can be done with all the moving around personally." She finishes.

"Wow, you would have thought he lived here his whole life and grew up around all of you. I feel drawn to him for some reason." I tell the girls honestly.

They both exchange looks before Sarah speaks.

"Look, we both know you are new here and are excited to meet new people and all but don't mess with Anthony. Cassie is a real bitch and is very territorial when it comes to Anthony. I honestly don't think he really truly loves her. I don't think they have a good relationship. But if you don't want to be Cassie's new target to belittle and hate you, then you need to just stay away from Anthony Taylor." They warn me.

Great. This sounds terrible. But I am going to listen to them. The last thing I want is to start drama after just moving here. Things are just starting to calm down to an extent and my life is falling into place. I will definitely be leaving Anthony Taylor alone and will ignore him as much as possible. He will be graduating at the end of this year so I only have to put up with it for the next 8 months. Ugh.

So I do as planned and continue to ignore Anthony over the next couple of weeks. I get to know Julie and Sarah even better as we spend a lot of time out of school together just as we do in school. But even though I don't look Anthony's way, I can feel his intense gaze on me at all times.

One day after school, I decide to take a walk around town to do a little shopping. We never really got to go back to school shopping before moving here and I really need some supplies. Plus we didn't know exactly what I needed for school so it only made sense to wait until I got here to see what was required for me to get. I put my headphones in as I walk through town and I look around noticing all the shops and buildings. I am really trying to learn my way around more. I am very deep in thought and distracted with my music. I hit the button at the traffic light to signal for me to walk. I look down at my phone to change the song but then look up to see that the WALK sign has been illuminated letting me know it is safe to cross. Or so I thought. I never even heard the screeching tires or the horn or let alone see the car barreling towards me. What I do feel is a huge collision with a body that tackles me to the ground before I am struck by the vehicle. I look up to see those same beautiful blue eyes that have been glaring at me since I have moved here. But he looks pissed. I suddenly remember I still have my headphones in and I reach to yank them out. Anthony jumps up abruptly not even bothering to help me up. I get up slowly and look at him to see him still scowling. What is his problem?

"Are you fucking stupid or do you just have a death wish?!" He asks me harshly.

Before I even get a chance to explain myself he begins to lecture me.

"You could have been killed! Didn't your parents teach you to look both ways before you crossed the street?! And to not be listening to headphones when you are walking on a busy roadway?!" He yells.

That's it. I am done with his attitude towards me. I am not going to sit here and take this.

"Look. For your information I hit the button and it lit up saying I was ok to walk. So I was paying attention. Obviously that driver wasn't because they had a red light. So you should be lecturing them! And the last time I checked who are you to say anything to me? You aren't my dad. My dad never talked to me this way when he was alive. Also, why the hell do you care? Ever since I moved here you act like I don't even exist. You give me dirty looks when I do look your way and have been nothing but a rude asshole!! People say you are popular but from where I stand I have absolutely no clue why?!" I yell back in anger.

I am fuming.

I start to walk away before I look back and finish my rant by saying, "Thanks for saving me but I have no clue why you did if you hate me that much. Look, I will stay out of your way and you stay out of mine for the rest of the school year. Have a nice life Anthony." I tell him bitterly before walking into the store and out of his sight.

I don't forget the look of complete shock on his face as I finish telling him off. Man that felt good. He needs to stop being such a jerk. Even if he did save my life. I feel a little guilty for a moment but I let that feeling subside. We just need to stay away from each other. He has anger issues and I don't want to be around him. I honestly don't see why people like him so much?!

Chapter 5- A Secret Revealed

Anthony's POV

    I storm into my house and run upstairs slamming my bedroom door behind me. God I am so mad at her!! She has gotten under my skin and I just can't let her go. Not again. I have tried so hard to push her away and just stay clear of her in general but it's getting harder and harder. She's so beautiful. She has grown into this gorgeous woman and I find it hard to keep my eyes off of her. Her body, her hair and sexy eyes. She is hot as fuck. And the way she stood up to me was such a turn on. It bothered me though what she said about her dad. I had no idea he had passed away. That really made me feel awful that I wasn't there for her. I liked her dad a lot.

But I have to keep my distance and it is slowly killing me inside. She was my best friend and my first ever crush. Although she never knew it at the time. I have never experienced a loss like Kendall. I don't think I can go through that again. I don't know how much longer I can keep my secret up. I have no clue how she will react when she finds out that I really am Seth. But I haven't been called that since I was 11. At least not in public anyway. That day we left Redbud was the day my entire life was turned upside down. No one knows and no one can ever know. It has to stay this this way. I am torn away from my thoughts when I hear the sound of my mom's voice outside my door.

"Come in ma!" I yell back.

"Anthony, are you ok? Why did you come in the house slamming doors?" She asks giving me a slight glare.

I haven't told her about Kendall coming back into my life. I don't know how she is going to react. But I think it might be time to.

"Did you have a fight with Cassie?" She asks when I don't respond.

I just scoff. Cassie can be so bitchy. I mean she's fun in certain ways but I just don't feel a spark with her. We have more of a physical connection.

"Mom, I need to tell you something. But I don't want you to freak out, ok?" I explain.

"Anthony I swear to God if you got her pregnant!!" She screams.

"What?? No ma! This has nothing to do with Cassie. Mom, what if I told you that Kendall just moved here and is now attending my school?" I ask cautiously.

She looks at me like she just saw a ghost.

"Oh my God!! This is not good. We are going to be found. Our secret is ruined. What are we going to do?!" She begins to panic.

"Mom, she thinks I am Anthony. The first day I saw her she thought it was me but I have fooled her. I treat her coldly like I can't stand the sight of her. And it's killing me." I say sadly.

It really is. She was my best friend. Probably the only real friend I ever had. She has walked back into my life and I have to act like she doesn't exist. I hate it.

"Sethy, I love you. I know this is hard but she can never know. No one can. If our secret ever gets out we are all as good as dead." She says solemnly.

I love it when she says my real name. It makes me feel like my life is like it used to be. Like it's real. That this fake charade of a life doesn't exist. I want normal again. I haven't had a normal life since I was 11. I so wish things had been different. That Kendall and I continued to grow up together and fell in love with each other eventually. That she was my girl and not Cassie. But unfortunately that's all just a dream.

"Mom, I promise I won't tell her anything. I will keep up this whole act. As much as it pains me to do so." I tell her.

"We have to be more careful now. I am glad you told me so I can disguise myself a little more out in public. If she sees me, she will know it's me. You have grown and changed but I haven't." She says seriously.

I never even thought about that part. I have to be more careful. This last year of school will be the worst one yet. I can't wait to move away from here next year. It can't come fast enough.

Author's Note:

So this was just so you can see Anthony AKA Seth's POV to get a little insight into what is going on with him. How many of you knew it was really Seth? I know he seems like an asshole but just wait until you get to know him more. Will he be able to stay away from Kendall? We will have to wait and see!!

Chapter 6-Weekend with Jordan

Kendall's POV

The next month of school flies by. I can't believe it's almost Halloween! I have continued to develop a friendship with Sarah and Julie. We spend time outside of school together, shopping, watching movies, and hanging out. I miss Jordan though. We try to talk as much as we can although with school, and his sports it makes it really hard to keep up with one another. We haven't seen each other in 2 months. He is going to come up to see me this weekend and I can't wait!! The girls and I decide to go shop for an outfit for me to wear and some Halloween costumes as well! There is a Halloween party we are going to go to next weekend and we are all looking forward to it.

As we shop around the numerous stores, I try on about 100 outfits. Everything is either way too tight or way too revealing. The girls are trying to get me to step out of my comfort zone and try something different. I am really trying but I refuse to compromise on some things. I decide I am trying on one more outfit and if I don't like it I am not getting anything new. I will just wear something I already have. The girls pick a sundress that's actually really cute. At least it looks cute on the hanger. We will see about what it looks like on me. I step back into the fitting room for the millionth time today and after slipping into the dress I close my eyes before turning around to look at myself in the mirror. I send up a quick silent prayer for this one to finally be the one. As I open my eyes, I am pleasantly surprised and relieved. It hugs my body in the right places, it's not too revealing, and it fits me nicely. We finally have a winner! After I show the girls we are all in agreement that this is the dress for my date with Jordan.

As soon as the weekend is here I am so excited to see Jordan I can't wait!! I run home after school to find Jordan talking with my mom on the couch. He decided to skip school today to make the long drive to see me! That way we have all evening and then all day tomorrow before he has to go back home on Sunday.

I run and jump in his arms as he gives me a very sweet and gentle kiss.

"I have missed you." He says smiling fondly at me.

"Same." I say smiling a little shyly.

As weird as it is I feel a little awkward around him suddenly. I guess it's just where we haven't seen each other in so long. At least not in person. I brush the feeling off as we all sit down and catch up for a bit.

Before long, Jordan and I head out to go to dinner and a movie. During dinner we catch up with one another. We talk about old memories and laugh at each other's stories. Then we head to the movies and we didn't watch about half of the movie. We were too busy making out in the back of the theater. Some dumb guys right behind us kept making stupid comments and cracking perverted jokes. So immature. As the closing credits roll on the screen and the lights begin to grow brighter, we get up and turn around to start heading out of the theater when I am met with those blue eyes that I have come to know so well and just can't seem to escape.

It was none other than Anthony along with his buddies. They were the ones right behind us in the theater making comments. I look to him wide eyed knowing I have been caught and may never hear the end of the teasing from these jocks, but the look I get back from him is not his normal cocky smirk. It was a look of pure anger. Why the hell is he angry? He looks over to Jordan sizing him up. Jordan is nowhere near as tall and built as Anthony so Anthony looks down to him. Jordan looks back and forth between us with confusion. The uncomfortable silence is killing me, so I decide to speak up.

"Jordan, these are some guys from my school. Guys this is Jordan, my boyfriend." I tell them.

Not that I owe them any explanations but standing here staring at one another was just too weird. At the mention of Jordan being my boyfriend I notice Anthony clench his teeth and make a fist with his hand. Seriously what the hell is the matter with him? One of his other buddies decides to chime in after I introduce Jordan.

"Damn Kendall you like getting freaky in the theater huh?" He asks.

I turn 10 shades of red. Jordan tries to speak up I am sure to defend me but I cut him off. It would be 3 against 1. Hardly a fair fight especially considering all of them are so much bigger than Jordan.

"Boys, have a nice rest of your weekend." I say quickly before pulling Jordan's arm to get us out of there as fast as possible.

Once we are in Jordan's car and on the way back to house he starts questioning me. Here we go. Ugh.

"Who were those guys back there?" He asks calmly.

One thing about Jordan is he isn't much of a shouter so I like that. He doesn't get hotheaded very easily. But I can tell he is irritated. Maybe even a little jealous.

"They go to my school. I don't know them very well. They are immature and dumb. I ignore them." I tell him honestly.

"Well the one big guy in the middle seemed really pissed off to see me with you. Is there something going on between you two?" He asks his voice laced with hurt.

Oh no. He couldn't be more wrong. I mean Anthony is hot as hell but he is an asshole. I would never go for him.

"You couldn't be more wrong. He has treated me like shit since I got here. He glares at me when I walk past him in the hallway, he makes rude comments and just is an absolute complete jerk. I have zero interest in him." I reply.

He seems a bit more relaxed at my response. We pull into my driveway and he puts the car in park and he turns to face me.

"Kendall, I really miss you. I know this is super hard us being apart. I still want to try to make it work but if you don't just please tell me. I don't want to make it harder if we prolong the inevitable. I am not sure if you still want to do this or not but I still want to." He says to me sincerely as he grabs my hand.

"Jordan, I still want that too. Nothing has changed. I still want to be with you I promise." I respond to him.

He smiles back at me sweetly. He gives me a sweet peck and we both head back into the house together.

The rest of the weekend flies by of course and we are back to school before I know it. I miss Jordan already. He was my comfort and source of familiarity that I longed for and missed. Although Julie and Sarah are great friends and I enjoy hanging out with them, I still miss my old life a lot. It was nice being in a school where everybody knew me and I had lots of friends. I stop at my locker after entering school and soon Julie and Sarah meet me to chat before we start our day. As we talk, I am interrupted by a guy clearing his voice from behind me. I look at the shocked facial expressions of my friends in front of me and know that whoever is behind me is not someone that normally talks to us. I turn around to see it's none other than Anthony Taylor standing there looking back at me with a half smirk. I don't like the looks of his expression at all. What is he up to?

Chapter 7-What Did I Agree To?

Kendall's POV

"What can I help you with Anthony?" I finally manage to blurt out after the initial shock wears off.

He looks back at me with an emotion I can't read before saying, "Do you girls mind if I talk to Kendall alone?" He says directed towards Julie and Sarah.

They just nod their heads and go to class.

"So..... I just wanted to say I am sorry for interrupting your date the other night and I am sorry for being an asshole to you when you first came here." He blurts out.

I look at him with a look of pure and utter shock I am sure.

"You're apologizing to me?" I ask flabbergasted.

"Yeah...I mean I don't know. Just trying to be nicer I guess." He says trying to sound more cool.

"You're forgiven." I say and smile at him.

He smiles back at me and I almost fainted right there at the sight. His smile could light up the darkest room. He has beautiful teeth and dimples.

"I do have to say one more thing..." he draws out as he leans down to whisper in my ear and gets dangerously close to me... "you would look a whole lot better standing next to a guy that is a lot taller, much more muscular, and could do things to you that most girls only dream about." He whispers seductively in my ear.

God that was hot. I think the temperature raised 100 degrees in here suddenly. I feel my face heat up from my blush and goosebumps pepper my skin. I can tell he notices it too. But soon I come back to reality and realize how cocky he just sounded. What is wrong with me? I decide to whisper my response back to him.

"Well Anthony, the problem is I don't know any guys like that. And Jordan is one hell of a guy. Don't judge a book by its cover. Have a nice day." I conclude as I smile and turn to walk away leaving Anthony standing with his mouth wide open in a complete state of shock.

Not today Satan. Not today.

I walk into class a few minutes late and I silently curse Anthony for making me tardy. Julie gives me a questioning look and I just quietly tell her that I will fill her in later. At lunch I tell both girls the whole story about running into Anthony in the movie theater and then I tell them all about what he said to me in the hallway. They both sit there with their jaws practically hitting the floor as I finish up my story. Julie is the first one to break their stunned silence.

"Kendall, do you realize that the most popular guy in this school, the one all the girls go crazy for and all the guys want to be like has a thing for you?" She asks me.

I look back at her and quickly shake my head.

"No, no he doesn't. He is just messing with me. Just continuing to be an asshole like he has been since I first moved here." I defend.

They are reading way too much into this.

"I dunno, I agree with Julie on this." Sarah says simply.

"I guess we will just agree to disagree on this one. Remember he has Cassie?" I tell them as I chuckle to myself.

They are crazy. Anthony is not interested in me at all. He just is trying to mess with my head and get under my skin. That's all this is. He's cocky and he's arrogant and I am going to mess with him as much as possible in return to put him in his place and bring his arrogance level down a notch.

The school day flies by quickly and soon enough I am walking home for the evening. Usually I do this in silence with only the thoughts in my head doing the talking but today was different. Someone has decided to tag along with me.

"Kendall, wait up!" I hear someone yell from behind me.

It's one of Anthony's friends. One of the guys that was at the movie theater with him the other night.

"It's Dylan, right?" I ask and he nods and smiles widely. Aww he is really cute. I never noticed it before.

"Did you need something?" I ask after a brief moment of awkward silence.

"Well...I was wondering if you would like to attend the big Halloween party that one of my buddies is having with me? You probably heard about it." He asks me. I stare back at him stunned.

"Well....I don't know. I mean I do have a boyfriend. The guy Jordan you saw at the theater the other night." I explain to him.

"Oh yeah, no this is just as friends. I want to get to know you better. You seem cool. Maybe we could start hanging out more?" He says to me.

This is really awkward and I really don't know what to think. I also don't know what to say. Before I can really think this over my mouth betrays me and blurts out "Sure."

Oh my God. What did I just do?

He smiles brightly back at me and says "Great! I will pick you up at 7:00 that night. Text me your address." He says as he jogs away from me.

I stutter trying to get the words out but I become completely tongue tied. What have I done? How will I explain this to the girls or worse to Jordan?? I feel like I am going to cheat on Jordan by going out with someone else. But he did say it was just as friends right?? So it's not even really a date. I find myself feeling completely conflicted and unsure of what to do. I quickly run home and call Sarah and Julie on Facetime. I explain the whole situation and they tell me they think he is going to make it like a date. Which is what I totally felt like it was too.

I instantly freak out. "Calm down." Julie says.

"What if I just don't tell him my address then he will never show up?" I ask unsure.

"That will never work. Number 1, he could just find your address another way. Number 2, he could also use that as a way to spread a bunch of crap around you at school saying God knows what." Sarah says.

She's right. Ugh I hate this.

"Listen, it's all good. We will come with you so it doesn't look like a date and he will get the hint that you are not interested." Julie says while smiling.

"That's perfect. Yes let's do that." I tell her. It's times like these I am so glad I met these girls.

Chapter 8-Halloween

Kendall's POV

It's the night of the Halloween party and I am very nervous. Not just because of this " friendly date" with Dylan but the fact that I will be at a party with a bunch of people from our school. Parties are social and I just don't know how to act around everyone. It's still hard being the new girl in school.

Julie and Sarah come over early to help me get ready and to get themselves ready for the party. We all have our costumes. We decided to be Monica, Rachel, and Phoebe from Friends. We came up with the idea together and I love it because it's one of my favorite shows of all time. I am Rachel, Julie is Monica, and Sarah is Phoebe. Our characters fit our personalities in many ways. We picked out clothes they would wear and even got wigs that we cut and styled to match them. After we are all dressed and ready and my mom snaps a couple hundred photos, we hear the doorbell ring and we head out to the party with Dylan.

On the way to the party I can tell Dylan is a little annoyed that I brought Sarah and Julie along. But he said this was a friend thing so I brought more friends. Ha! We arrive at the party and things have already begun. Lots of beer and liquor everywhere, people dancing and grinding up on each other, kids making out on couches and in hallways. These poor people's house!! My mom would kill me if I did this!

As we come into the main party area, we all grab drinks. The girls each grab a beer, Dylan takes a few shots, and I decide to take the safe route and drink some of the punch. I am not a drinker. At least not yet anyway. After hanging out for a bit and having a few drinks, we all are loosened up and decide to go hit the dance floor. Julie and Sarah dance together, while Dylan and I pair off as well. Dylan is actually a good dancer. He have fun dancing for a while until I suddenly feel a harsh tap on my shoulder. I turn around to see Anthony glaring between Dylan and I . Geez why does he always seem so pissed off?

"Can I talk to you for a minute?" He asks me motioning for me to join him away from the dance floor.

I just nod my head and follow him. Why do I feel like a lecture is coming on?

"What happened to Jordan? Why are you here with Dylan?" He says venomously especially as he says Dylan's name.

"Ummm, not that it is any of your business but he invited me and my friends here as friends and nothing else. I made it clear to him that I was taken by Jordan." I say as smoothly as I can.

I feel a little off. Must be all the dancing I have been doing. Making me dehydrated. I decide to walk over and get some more punch. Anthony of course follows me after he lets off a huge scoff.

"Are you really that nieve? Dylan only wants one thing from you and that isn't friendship. He thinks with his dick. Trust me." He says bluntly.

I open my mouth out of shock and anger. "How dare you!! You have no right to say anything to me and you have no idea. Plus why do you care? Cassie is over there, why aren't you with your girlfriend?" I ask feeling livid.

He just looks back at me angrily until he finally turns around and walks off in the direction of Cassie. Thank God. Such an ass I swear. I go back over to find the girls and Dylan still dancing where I left them. We dance for a while longer making us develop an insatiable thirst, so we continue to down drinks. After a while, Sarah says she isn't feeling well. Julie goes with her to try and find a bathroom in this place. Leaving me alone with Dylan. He asks me if I want to go outside with him to get some fresh air and to get away from the loud music for a little bit. I agree. I need a break. My ears ring for a few moments at the newfound quiet that the October night brings.

"You know you look really pretty tonight. Way prettier than Rachel ever was." Dylan says to me.

Ok that was kind of cheesy but I just laugh and say "thanks." I suddenly feel a little wobbly probably from all the dancing we have been doing and I lose my footing and fall right into Dylan's arms. He takes this as a sign that I am trying to kiss him and he begins devouring my lips with very sloppy kisses. Yuck. He is the worst kisser ever. Gross. I push away from him breaking the kiss for a moment.

"Come on baby, I saw how much action you were giving your man in the theater. Can I get in on some of that and maybe take it a step further?" He asks before grabbing me against him roughly pinning my arms in the process.

I don't know what is wrong with me but it's like I can't use my senses correctly. I try to scream and tell him no and to stop but he keeps trying to grope me and kiss me no matter how much I protest. I finally send up a silent prayer for someone to come rescue me and as if God answered me right then, I feel Dylan's body being ripped away from me. I stand there in a state of shock as I look at Anthony who is now glaring at Dylan.

Holy crap I thought he gave me dirty looks. If looks could kill, Dylan would be 6ft under right now.

"What the fuck are you doing to her?!!" Anthony screams at Dylan.

"I was just having fun, trying to get her to loosen up." He says trying to defend his actions.

"Oh really? Well the last time I checked "no" and "stop" mean to cut it out and why the fuck would you even try something like that when you both are drunk?" He booms.

What? I haven't drank.

"I'm not drunk. I haven't drank any alcohol." I say in my defense.

He looks at me like I am an idiot. "I saw you drinking the punch." He says to me through gritted teeth.

I sit there confused for a few moments before realization hits me. Oh the punch was spiked? No wonder I feel so out of it. Crap. I am torn from my thoughts when I hear Anthony continue to yell at Dylan.

"Now get the fuck out of here before I beat your bitch ass!!" He yells at Dylan and that's all if takes for Dylan to take off running.

I look down to the ground in complete embarrassment. I notice there was a bit of a crowd drawn around at the sound of all the commotion. Then I hear Cassie yelling at Anthony from beside him as he stares at me intensely.

"Anthony I don't know why you even care?! Take me home now!!" She demands him.

After a few moments he finally looks her way and they walk to his car and get in and drive off. I make my way back inside and find Sarah and Julie. Julie informs me Sarah got sick and they need to go. I decide to call a cab to come get us since we lost our ride and none of us are in any shape to drive obviously even if we wanted to. After getting back to my house, we don't even discuss the events of the night because we are all just so exhausted. We give in to our tiredness and fall into a deep sleep.

Chapter 9- Rachel Was Always My Favorite

Kendall's POV

I wake up with a throbbing headache. Is this what they call a hangover? No wonder people complain about them. I look over to see the girls are still passed out. Yeah I am not a fan of drinking just yet. I gently wake them up and we all head downstairs to find the cure for a hangover. We each get some Tylenol and water, and I make us a nice breakfast. By the time we finish eating, we are all starting to feel a lot better. We start talking about the events of last night.

"I can't believe that jerk Dylan tried to pull that crap with you! Drunk or not it wasn't cool." Julie says as Sarah agrees with her.

"I guess I should have expected something like that. He thinks I am easy or something just because he saw me making out with Jordan. I should have never done that in a public place. That wasn't like me. I just missed Jordan so much." I tell them.

After a few moments of silence Sarah asks a question.

"Have you and Jordan....you know?" She trails off and Julie perks up at that question.

"Actually no we haven't. We have done other things but not that yet. I am just not ready. What about you guys?" I ask taking the attention off of me.

They both shake their head no in unison. Glad to know we all have that in common.

"Anthony sure was protective of you though." Julie states with a smirk.

"He just confuses me so badly. He has these small moments of kindness and then he has this cockiness/arrogance about him. His mood swings are terrible. Plus he has a girlfriend so I have no clue why he has any interest in my life anyway?!" I tell them honestly.

"Sometimes crushes are hard and you can have a lot of complex emotions." Sarah adds.

"Crush?" I laugh out loud. "He doesn't have a crush on me." I say in disbelief.

"I think you must be blind." Julie says.

"What do you mean?" I ask honestly.

"Well the way he looks at you. He has never looked at a girl that way before. Not even Cassie. And he flirted with you blatantly in front of everyone in the school knowing it would get back to Cassie." Julie reasons.

My heart flutters a little during her explanation. Why? I am not interested in Anthony and I have Jordan. Why do I care what he thinks? I think for a moment before answering.

"I just don't see it, I am sorry. You guys told me to stay away from him and I have tried. He keeps coming around. But now I have to at least thank him for keeping Dylan in check during the party last night." Ugh.

I hate having to apologize. It's just something I am not good at. Not that I don't feel sorry when I make mistakes, it's just hard for me to apologize. I feel awkward and never know what to say. I talk to the girls a little more about it and they give me some ideas. We spend the rest of the day hanging out before having to get ready to go to school tomorrow and face Anthony.

As I walk into the building, I immediately begin scanning the room for Anthony. I want to get this whole apology over with. I look over to Cassie's locker which I normally see them both standing at every morning but I don't see either of them. Are they not here today? That's odd not to see them together. I begin looking around the hallways until I find Anthony standing with some of his buddies. I see Dylan and I notice he has a black eye?? How did that happen. He looks at me and immediately looks away and walks off. Great. Now that's going to be one more awkward thing to deal with. But my focus is Anthony. I tap on his shoulder and he turns around and looks at me with a look of slight shock and then he puts a scowl back on his face. He immediately starts to walk away ignoring me completely. So rude.

"So I guess you aren't going to talk to me." I say as I follow behind him.

No response. Ok that answers that.

"Look Anthony I just want to apologize to you for being so rude when you were just trying to give me a warning about Dylan. I am sorry I didn't listen to you. I should have. Had you not come out there I don't know what might have happened and that scares me." I say honestly getting a little choked up.

I hadn't planned on getting that in depth with this apology but I just can't help myself. I feel like I could tell him anything. He turns around at my brutal honesty.

"Well you don't ever have to worry about Dylan again. I took care of it." He says seriously.

I realize he means that he punched Dylan and my eyes go wide.

"I didn't want you to punch him, but I am glad you scared him off. He really gave me bad vibes after all of that happened." I tell him.

"Well I am glad I could help." He says with a tight lipped smile. Now there is awkward silence.

"Well have a good day." I tell him as I go to turn around and head to class.

But he grabs my arm and it stops me.

"Listen, I am definitely not a Dylan, and probably not a Jordan, but I want you to give me a chance. Go on a date with me." He says.

What?? There goes the fluttering of my heart. Stop it. Just calm down. You already have a boyfriend and he has a girlfriend?! Wait. This is nuts.

"What about Cass...." I don't even get the question out before he interrupts,

"We broke up. The other night at the party actually. I found out she cheated on me and to be honest we just weren't very compatible." He tells me.

"Ok, but Jordan..." again he stops me but this time he grabs both of my arms pulling me closer to him. He looks deeply into my eyes and I feel like the air has been taken from my lungs and the world has stopped. It's just the two of us in this whole school. I have never felt this way before. It's very strange.

"I know you feel that too. I am drawn to you Kendall. I can't help it. You're beautiful and I have tried to stay away from you because I was with Cassie and I knew you were off limits since you were with Jordan,'but I just can't resist you anymore. Please go out with me. Just one date and if you have a terrible time then we will both go our separate ways and that will be it." He convinces me.

Why do these boys have this effect on me? But again before I can really think about my answer, I blurt out "Ok." I really need to get that under control.

He smirks back at me and tells me, "I'll pick you up at 7:30 on Friday."

I just smile back at him, still in shock and unable to speak. I go to turn away and head down the hallway to class when he says, "Oh and by the way....Rachel was always my favorite FRIEND's character." He smirks at me and I just blush profusely back at him before finally heading to class. What is he doing to me??!

Chapter 10-Torn Between Them

Kendall's POV

I can't believe that just happened. Now I am currently in Trigonometry and I can't even focus at all. All I can think about is Anthony. And Jordan. What am I going to do? I still really care about Jordan. But I feel some type of attraction to Anthony and I just don't understand it. I need to figure it out. But I don't know how to tell Jordan or even if I should tell him? I am majorly conflicted. Suddenly I get a text. Who could this be during school?

Can you send me your address? I can pick you up at your house? From unknown contact

How the hell did Anthony already get my phone number?? Julie!!! She had to have given it to him. I have to yell at her later. I hurry up and text back quickly.

Sounds good. I will text you my address later ;)

I respond quickly so I don't get caught texting in class. The rest of the day goes by in a flash and I catch Anthony giving me a few smirks in the hallways when I see him. I can also feel his gaze when I am not looking. This time it's not the normal glare though.

When I get home, I call the girls instantly to talk to them about everything. I kept it very minimal at lunch I told them I would go into greater detail later. I didn't want any listening ears to spread rumors.

"Girls, I feel horribly guilty. I just don't know about this. I should cancel right?" I ask.

"No!! Are you crazy? Just listen. Just go on one date. Don't tell Jordan anything yet. Wait and see how this date goes. If it doesn't go well, then no harm done. Don't even tell Jordan and just go back to the way things were. But if it goes well, then you need to be honest with Jordan and just tell him you have feelings for someone else too." Julie says.

Ugh. This really sucks. I really like Jordan. But when I am near Anthony I feel a strong connection to him and I just can't ignore it. It's so hard but I know Julie is right.

"Ok. You're right. That's what I will do. Thank you girls for all of your advice as always. Not sure what I would do with out you two." I tell them sincerely.

The rest of the week flies by and by the time school ends on Friday and I get home, I am feeling very nervous. The girls come over and help me get ready for the date and then leave me to sit and internally freak out until Anthony gets here. My mom isn't here to talk to either. She had to work late tonight. I still just feel so guilty and wrong going on this date. My thoughts are suddenly interrupted by the phone ringing. Oh no it's Jordan.

"Hey!" I answer probably at little too eagerly.

"Hey, what are you doing?" He asks.

"Oh nothing. What are you doing?" I ask in return.

"Nothing. Why haven't you been calling me lately?"

He asks. Oh gosh. I hate not being honest with him.

"I am sorry. I have just been busy lately. I miss you." It's true. Jordan has always been one of my best friends.

"I love you." He says and I almost have a heart attack.

He has never said that before to me. Do I love him? I mean I do care for him but do I love him?

"What?" I ask in complete shock.

"I love you. I have been wanting to say it for a while now. You don't have to say it back." He says.

"Ok. Thank you. I mean I care about you so much." I say unsure of what to say.

"Well I guess I will talk to you later." He says his voice laced with sadness.

"Yeah. I will call you tomorrow." I tell him as we hang up.

Now my heart feels like it just broke into a million pieces. I really should cancel this date. The sudden ring of the door bell breaks me from my thoughts and causes my heart rate to increase. Shit. Now I have to go down there and tell AnthonyI am not going on this date with him. I guess I am going to upset two guys tonight. Ugh. I rapidly head down the steps and open the front door.

The sight in front of me takes my breath away. Anthony is standing there with a beautiful bouquet of flowers, with the best smile on his face. And he looks....hot. I shamelessly check him out and he catches me and instantly gives me a smirk. My face turns pink from embarrassment.

"Like what you see?" He asks knowing that will turn my face even redder which it does. I give him a nice slap on the arm and he just laughs.

"Are you ready to go?" He asks. I shake my head yes and before I know it we are heading out down the road in his car. As we ride, I realize that I was going to cancel this date until he came to the door and distracted me with his good lucks. Damnit he is good.

It's not long before we arrive at our first stop. It's a really nice restaurant. We head inside and order before we begin to talk. I want to know more about him. He intrigues me.

"So, tell me about your family?" I ask. He looks at me wide eyed.

Ok that was odd.

"My family...well Umm...I have a brother that is older and doesn't live at home anymore. My dad is in the military and is gone all the time and my mom doesn't work. She stays at home with me. We have moved around a lot my entire life. Once I graduate though, I think she and my dad will move away to be closer to my grandparents. I plan to go to college in Texas so I won't exactly be home much." He answers.

My heart hurts a little when he says he is moving so far away after graduation. But wait...why do I care??

"So what about you??" He asks breaking me from my thoughts.

"I am an only child and my dad passed away about 10 months ago. It was really hard. My mom had always stayed at home, so she had to get a job thus is why we moved here. Better job opportunities and plus I think she wanted to move away from the town that will constantly remind her of my dad." I explain.

He just silently shakes his head in understanding.

"I am so sorry. I know...I mean I am sure he was a great man." He says kindly.

"Thank you. It's been hard but it's getting a little easier. I just don't want to leave my mom. She is all alone." I tell him honestly.

We spend more time getting to know each other throughout our meal and then he takes me on adventures. He takes me sight seeing at places I had never been since being here, then he takes me to a roller skating rink which was a blast. We laugh hysterically at one another when we fall. We then end up at the drive in movie where we watch one of my favorite movies. After the movie, he drives me home.

As we pull into the driveway, I say to him, "I want to say thank you for tonight. I really had a lot of fun I have to admit." I tell him shyly.

I really did have so much fun. I probably haven't had this much fun since I was a kid and Seth and I went on adventures. He really reminds me of him.

As if he can tell I am having an internal conversation, he asks "What are you thinking about?" I don't know why I feel so comfortable around him but I do.

It's like I have known him my whole life. "It's just that you remind me of someone. My best friend from childhood. I miss him so much. When he left, it broke my heart. It took me a long time to get over it." I tell him honestly.

I don't think I will ever be completely over it. Anthony then does something completely and totally unexpected. He moves in and devours my lips in a very heated kiss.

Chapter 11- First Kiss

Kendall's POV

Here I am kissing Anthony and when I say it's amazing...it's AMAZING!! Never have I ever felt this way. Even with Jordan. This is hot and passionate. My heart is beating wildly in my chest and my stomach is doing somersaults. Not to mention what it's doing to my loins. It's so hot in here! He takes his tongue and licks my bottom lip asking for entrance which I grant. He deepens the kiss and I have to stop him long enough to take a breath.

"I am so sorry. I got carried away... I just really like you..." he stutters out.

"It's ok Anthony. I mean I kissed you back. And I would be lying if I said I didn't like it." I say as I blush and he just smirks.

He leans in to kiss me again but I have to stop it this time. I put my hand up and place it on his chest.

"However...I still have a boyfriend Anthony. Remember Jordan? And I have to figure all of this out. I have feelings for you but I have feelings for Jordan still too. I can't just brush that aside. I have been with him for a year." I explain.

He goes back to the scowl on his face that I grew so used to seeing when I first met him. He is pouting. Aww...it's cute. But I don't let him see me smile.

"If only things were different and...nevermind." He says under his breath.

I look at him confused for a moment.

"I gotta go." He says quickly.

"Ok. Thanks for this evening." I tell him.

"Yeah whatever." He says as I get out.

I look back at him hurt but I see the same hurt in his eyes. He quickly looks away and backs out of the driveway hurriedly and speeds off down the road. Ugh. Well I did manage to hurt 2 guys tonight. Two guys I care about. What am I going to do?? I walk inside and my mom is watching tv on the couch.

"Oh hi, honey how was your date?" She asks.

"I am so confused mom. I like Jordan a lot. He even told me he loved me earlier!" I start to tell her.

"He what?!!!" She interrupts me.

"Woah mom hold on. I didn't say it back because I don't know if I have those strong of feelings for him. I care about him deeply I really do. But I don't know if I love him. Then I go out on this date with Anthony and I am starting to have feelings for him too. I don't know what to do. I don't want to hurt anyone and I hate feeling so torn." I tell her honestly.

"Look honey, I know exactly what you are saying. But you have to stop worrying about hurting someone. You need to really think about your feelings and you should only pursue things with the guy that means something to you in the sense that you can't imagine not being with them. That you feel your heart break at the thought of never seeing them again. That's love. And until you know that feeling than just have fun and explore things with both guys. But I think you should be honest with Jordan and tell him you are talking to someone else. It's only fair." She says.

She is right. No matter what I need to be honest. It's eating away at me.

I go upstairs and call Jordan and tell him everything. It was so hard. A lot of shed tears between us and him being really mad. I told him he could date other people as well but he was not ok with that. We basically ended the phone call not on a good note. But I at least feel relieved that I came clean. After I get off the phone with Jordan, I decide to get ready for bed as my exhaustion from tonight and this week is catching up to me. I am laying in bed watching a movie on Netflix trying to relax until I fall asleep, when a ding from my phone indicating that I have a text message gets my attention. I grab my phone and read the text.

I am sorry for being an asshole. I knew you were with Jordan before going on this date. I wasn't fair to you. But it's hard for me. The more I am around you, the more I like you and I feel sorta jealous I guess. But anyway I will leave you alone so you can be with Jordan. See you around.-Anthony

I think for a few moments before I begin to text him back.

Anthony. I really like you. And I just talked to Jordan when I got home this evening and I told him everything. Well other than the fact that we kissed,but I feel better telling him. I still want to get to know you and even go out more if you want to. I just need to explore my feelings a bit to see who I really want to be with. Just give me a little time. Please.

I wait for him to respond. After a couple of minutes my phone dings again.

That's fair. See you Monday at school.

That silly little text and emoji makes my heart flutter. Why do I feel this way with him? It's just different. I quickly text him goodnight and I fall asleep thinking about Anthony and Jordan. How will I ever figure this out??

Chapter 12- What Is This Girl Doing To Me?

Anthony's POV

I can't believe what this girl is doing to me. I have never felt this way. I mean I have cared about her since I was 5 years old, but I never thought I would have these kind of feelings towards her. And I can't leave her alone. I promised my mom I would and I hate going against what she wants. But I am so drawn to her. We are meant to be together. Fate brought her back to me. I am not losing her again. Not even to Jordan. I don't care. If she has feelings for me too like she says she does, then I have to convince her that I am the one for her. She just can't ever figure out who I really am. And I have to keep her away from my mom because then they will both know the truth and I will be dead.

I walk into school Monday morning and instantly go to look for Kendall. Before I can get to her, Cassie stops me in the hallway. Fuck. Here we go.

"I can't believe you dumped me for that bitch. Yeah people saw you together this weekend and it got back to me." She seethes at me.

"Look Cassie. You can have any guy you want in this school. You don't need me. We aren't that compatible. I mean you cheated on me last year. I forgave you but I just am not interested anymore. I am going to move on and you should too." I tell her.

"But I don't want any other guy I want you!!!! She screams at me getting the attention of everyone in the hallway. Shit.

"I gotta go. I am not doing this here." I tell her as I storm off.

I gotta get Cassie interested in someone else to get her off my back. Maybe she will like Jordan so I can be with Kendall? Wishful thinking. I don't get a chance to see Kendall before my first class so I go ahead and head in. I will catch her after this.

My first class crawls by, but as soon as the bell rings I dart out of the room to go find her. I know her schedule by heart. Not to sound like a creeper or anything but I have watched her since the first day she stepped into this school. I know her daily routine. I wait for her outside her class. I hear her talking to Julie inside and they walk out together. When her eyes meet mine she smiles widely. I can't help but smile back at her. Her smiles are infectious. I check her out shamelessly. She's 5ft 3. So tiny. But she's curvy in all the right ways. She has long blonde hair and beautiful blue/gray eyes. She's breathtakingly gorgeous. I walk up to her.

"Hi!" She says eagerly.

"Hey." I say back.

Julie excuses herself from our conversation.

"Can I take you home after school today? I notice you always walk." I tell her.

"Sure." She smiles.

"Cool. I will meet you outside then after." I say.

"See you then." She replies.

She starts to walk away but before she can I grab her arm and swing her back around so she is in my arms. I lean down and give her a chaste kiss on her lips. As small of a gesture as that was, it makes my heart skip a beat. She blushes and bites her lip. Fuck that was such a turn on. I love making her blush. I smirk at her and she blushes even more. She walks away and I can't help but stare. I hate to see her go, but I love to watch her leave.

After school I meet her and take her home like I promised. Before she gets out of the car I lean in and give her a slow, but passionate kiss.

I pull away to tell her, "If you don't want me to kiss you, I won't. But I just have a hard time controlling myself around you." I tell her as I tuck a stray hair behind her ear.

She smiles and bites her lip again.

"You gotta stop biting that lip. It makes me wanna do things to you that I know we aren't ready for yet." I tell her huskily and I have never seen her face turn so red.

"I'll text you later." I tell her and she just nods and heads inside.

Later on that evening, I text her telling her that I would see her tomorrow and that I was sorry if I made her feel uncomfortable. She told me not to worry about it that she just gets embarrassed easily. This girl is going to be the death of me.

Chapter 13- Surprise Visit

Kendall's POV

The next couple of months fly by. Anthony and I have grown closer and I have to say I have really enjoyed getting to know him. He's funny, and good looking and very good at showing affection. That is one thing Jordan didn't do a lot of. Maybe he didn't like PDA, but Anthony doesn't care. He loves to kiss me just about everywhere and anywhere he can. By anywhere I mean physical places not body parts. Get your mind out of the gutter.

My mom and I decide to invite Anthony over for dinner which he accepted. He hasn't met her yet because most of our interaction has been at school. I can't wait to see what her impression of him is. So here we are currently waiting for him to arrive. A knock at the door breaks me from my thoughts. I rush to answer it and am greeted by a handsome guy literally sweeping me off my feet while bringing me up to his height to give him a kiss. It's the little things like that, that I love.

We head to the kitchen where my mom is cooking away and I introduce her to Anthony. Soon we are sitting down to eat. Mom asks Anthony questions trying to find out more about him.

She then turns to me about halfway through the meal and says "You were right. He really does remind me of Seth."

Right as she says this, Anthony knocks his glass over spilling his drink everywhere. We get up to clean it up and hear a knock at the door. Who could that be? I go open the door, only to find Jordan standing on my doorstep. Oh shit.

He walks inside and I instantly feel extremely awkward. Both guys I like and care about are here. In the same room. They stare each other down. Yikes. Jordan and I have only talked a few times since he told me he loved me. I am honestly shocked he didn't just break up with me when I told him about Anthony. But I guess love makes you do crazy things. For instance, showing up at your girlfriend's house 5 hours away unannounced.

"Jordan, what are you doing here?" I ask him my voice full of shock and surprise.

"I wanted to see you. I missed you." He says as he hugs me.

I look over to Anthony to see him glaring now at Jordan. I have seen that look before. It was the look he gave Dylan that night at the Halloween party. Shit. This is not good. I see him clench his fists at his side.

"Jordan, can you excuse us for a moment please?" I ask him. He nods and goes over to talk to my mom.

I grab Anthony and bring him into my room shutting the door behind us.

"Anthony, I swear I didn't know..." is all I am able to get out before he devours my lips. I pull away.

"Anthony. Jordan's in the next room." I tell him out of breath.

"Do you want me to stop?" He asks as he leans in and cages me against my bedroom door.

He then starts sucking on my neck. It feels amazing. He trails kisses all the way down from my ear to right below my chin.

"Mmmmm" is all I manage to get out. My mind is foggy. He does this to me. Wait we need to talk. I come to my senses long enough to put my hand to his chest pushing him back.

"Anthony, I know this is hard. I am trying really hard to make a decision here." I say.

"Yeah, and I am helping you decide." He says as he goes to lean in towards my neck again.

I have to stop him before I get in a trance for the second time tonight. I dart away under his arms and across the room.

"You play dirty Anthony." I say and he smirks.

"And before you can come up with some perverted response to that, I just need to say that I didn't invite Jordan but maybe him being here will help me make my decision. Spending time with both of you will really help me choose." I explain to him.

I see some hurt flash through his eyes before he lowers them to the ground.

"Fine. I am going to go. Spend time with him and call me when you want to do something." He says to me and he goes to leave but before he can I grab his arm and pull him back to me placing a chaste kiss on his lips.

He smiles back at me and then leaves and I hear the front door shut.

I walk back out into the living room to see my mom and Jordan talking.

"This was quite the surprise, wasn't it sweetheart?" Mom asks me.

"Yes. It was." I say not really knowing what else to talk about.

"Well, I will leave you two alone." Mom says as she walks out of the room.

Thanks mom. Now it can be even more awkward.

"I didn't expect to see him here with you. Things are moving kind of fast between you two." He says with his voice laced with disgust.

"Jordan, he is staying home alone. His mom went to stay with his grandma in Maine, but Anthony couldn't go because he has to start practice this weekend and his mom wanted to spend 2 weeks up there with her. So he stayed behind. His dad is in the military and is deployed. My mom wanted to meet him and thought it would be a nice gesture." I explain.

He just nods his head in understanding not caring to discuss it anymore.

"Well, I came here to see you and to take you out on the town. Your mom and I were just talking while you were in there with him and she said I can sleep on the couch tonight and then we can spend the day together tomorrow." He says.

"Sounds like fun." I smile at him.

We talk for a little while catching up with one another and then we all decide to go to bed. I change into my pajamas, brush my teeth and snuggle into bed. I have just dozed off when I feel a dip in my bed. I wake up to see Jordan laying in front of me. He then slowly moves in and grabs my face before devouring my lips like his life depended on it. This kiss is very needy. Not like any I have ever felt with him. He makes his way over close to me and climbs on top of me kissing me deeply. I pull away to get air.

"What was that for?" I ask him.

"I want to show you what you have been missing." He says before kissing me again.

This time it's more urgent. He begins to take his hand and rub it over my breasts for a few moments as he deepens the kiss. He then begins to trail his hands further south. So Jordan and I have never had sex but we have done other things together. I guess he is trying to pick back up where we left off?!

"Jordan, maybe we should stop?" I tell him.

"Why? You never stopped me before? I just miss you and I want to show you how much I love you." He says.

God he said he loved me again. And I just don't know what to say back. He starts to kiss me again and feel me up. I push his hand away when it heads south again.

"Why are you acting so distant? Are you screwing that Anthony guy or something?" He asks frustrated.

"What?! No! I can't believe you would say that?!"' I tell him.

"Well, I don't know what to think anymore. You are so distant. I really can't stand the idea of you with this other guy to be honest." He says.

"I know and I hate doing this to both of you. I know it's not fair and I need to figure things out." I tell him honestly.

"Well let's just see how this weekend goes and enjoy our time together." He says.

He holds me close to him and I drift off to sleep. My last thoughts before I fall asleep are how different kissing Jordan is compared to kissing Anthony. They are worlds different. And I am really not sure what that means just yet. I feel safe with Jordan and comfortable because we have been together so long. But with Anthony, he makes me feel excited and makes my heart race. I have to make a choice and I am leaning more one way than the other.

Chapter 14- I Know Who I Am Choosing

Kendall's POV

I wake up remembering that I fell asleep in Jordan's arms. He must have gotten up after I fell asleep. I am sure he didn't want mom to catch us together. She would kill me! I walk downstairs to see Jordan and mom talking while mom makes us breakfast. We sit and enjoy it before Jordan takes me out on our adventure he planned for us.

He took me to see a movie and then we had a picnic in the park afterwards. After that we walked around the mall shopping and having a few laughs at some of the things we see. It was a really fun day.

Jordan has to get up early and leave the next morning and we say our good byes. For some reason it just isn't hurting as much this time to say good bye. It's very weird.

Later on that afternoon, I get a text from Anthony asking me if Jordan had left yet. When I told him he had, he asked if I wanted to go somewhere with him this evening. He said it was a surprise. I agree to go with him and before long he is picking me up. As we ride in the car, he reaches over and grabs my hand. The feeling it gives me sends goosebumps up my arm. Why don't I feel that way when Jordan touches me? It's weird. We finally reach our destination. We are parked outside a large brick building on the outskirts of the city.

"Close your eyes." He tells me and I do so as he walks me inside.

I hear lots of noise and when he tells me to open them I am completely shocked and excited. He took me to see my favorite band in concert!!! I scream and jump up and down thanking him for taking me. We have front row seats and we have a blast singing and dancing along. Then he takes me out for dinner afterwards to one of my favorite restaurants around here. We laugh and have a great night together.

We pull back in my driveway and I suddenly get the courage to ask him something I have been wanting to ask him.

"Are you a virgin?" I blurt out.

Geez nice going Kendall. Not exactly how I planned to get to that question.

"Well...I am not going to lie to you no I am not. Why are you?" He asks me.

I don't respond but just look at him embarrassed.

"There is nothing to be embarrassed about. That's a good thing. I figured you and Jordan already had." He says the last part with annoyance.

I can tell that thought was not one he enjoyed.

"We have done other things...but not that." I say.

He looks at me with a mixture of emotions. Anger that Jordan and I had done more than just kiss, but most of all he looks at me with lust.

"I have never even had an orgasm with Jordan." I blurt out again.

Boy the word vomit just keeps coming out. He looks at me with a smirk.

"You mean to tell me he has never pleased you before?" He asks cockily.

"Look, it's not as easy as you think and it's not a competition." I say.

"I think that sounds like a challenge." He says to me.

I look at him confused for a moment before he grabs me and pulls me on top of him. He pulls me impossibly close to him as he kisses me with more intensity than ever before.

"Listen, we better stop. I will get carried away." He says breathlessly.

"What if I want you to?" I ask him.

"Fuck." He curses before kissing me again this time a little more slowly.

"I don't want to do anything right here. Let's go to my house since my mom isn't home. Just text your mom and say you will be back in a bit that you forgot something at the restaurant." He says.

I do as he says my heart racing. My adrenaline is through the roof. I can't believe I said the things I said to him. God I hope I don't regret this later. We pull into his driveway and head into his house. He quickly pulls me upstairs and into his bedroom. He kisses me slowly at first and then becomes more needy and urgent. He lays me down on the bed and he begins to suck on my neck again like he did at my house the other night.

"That feels so goooooddd." I moan out.

"You like that baby?" He asks.

"Mmmmmm." I say in response.

"Fuck me." He curses before kissing me hard on the lips.

Our tongues intertwine together as I feel him begin to put his hand up my shirt. He teases my buds with his fingers and I instantly feel them become hard. Oh my God that feels so good. He then unhooks my bra and sneaks his hand up underneath to touch my bare skin. He begins to twist my nipples between his fingers ever so lightly and I instantly feel a surge of excitement building in my stomach. Oh my God the way he makes me feel. It never felt like this with Jordan. I then feel him unbutton my pants, but as he does so he looks me in my eyes and silently asks me for permission. I nod yes. I then feel his large fingers begin to touch me and I can't believe what I have been missing. He instantly finds my clit and begins massaging it with his thumb while inserting another finger in me. The sensation is like nothing I have ever felt. I moan loudly with pleasure as he continues his assault on my pussy. I can feel my orgasm building in my belly and as if he reads my mind he speeds up just enough to send me over the edge. I cry out loudly as I have the first orgasm someone has given me. He kisses me softly as I come down from my high.

"Where did you, how did you....?" Is all I can mutter out due to being out of breath.

"Fuck that was hot watching you get off. You are a sight to see." He says smirking at me knowing he embarrassed me.

He kisses me again and I feel his hard cock against my leg.

He looks down as he notices me looking and says "It's fine. It will go away in a few minutes." He says.

Obviously not expecting something in return. But I would never do that to him. I have done this before with Jordan and unlike with me I have given him many orgasms. It's kind of hard to fake those if you are a guy. I am not an expert by any means, but this isn't my first hand job. I reach down unbuttoning his pants slowing as I sneak my hand into his boxers. Holy fuck he has a huge dick. Way bigger than Jordan. Not that I am comparing or anything. I begin stroking it slowly up and down with my hands gripped firmly around.

"Oh God baby yes." He moans out.

Ok I guess that means he likes it. I continue to stroke it repeatedly getting faster with each movement and before long he is coming undone.

"Fuck Kendall. You drive me wild." He says breathlessly.

I blush at him. We both lay down next to each other and kiss each other softly.

"How come it feels different with you?" I ask as I break the kiss.

"What do you mean?" He asks.

"Well it's hard to explain but every time I am with you and you touch me or you kiss me I feel goosebumps, my heart beat races, and my stomach flutters. I have never really felt that with Jordan. I mean I liked to kiss him and all but it just feels totally different with you." I tell him honestly.

"I feel that way about you too. Like something draws me to you. I think it just means we have strong feelings for each other." He tells me.

God. I know now who I am choosing. The realization hits me like a ton of bricks. I felt safe with Jordan and I like him because he's a good guy and my first boyfriend and first kiss. But I never felt the way I feel with Anthony and I never will. I am falling for Anthony. I need to let Jordan go.

Chapter 15- Mrs. Tarantino?

Kendall's POV

    Now I know that I can't keep things going with Jordan. I have stronger feelings for Anthony. It's going to hurt me so much to break his heart. But I just can't keep going like this. It's not fair to either guy and it's not fair to me. I will hate it that I will most likely lose my friendship with Jordan because of this but it just has to be this way.

I call Jordan and after an hour of a very painful conversation, we end the call. It was very awkward. He cried and I cried but in the end we both agreed that we needed to break up. I hope he finds someone that makes him happy and cares about him, the way I do for Anthony. He deserves that.

I haven't told Anthony about this yet. I am going to surprise him later by going to his house and telling him, now that I know where he lives.

I spend the day catching up with my school work and watching some of my favorite movies. When it comes time for me to get ready to go over there, I suddenly become so nervous. What if he doesn't feel the same way about me? I shake these thoughts from my head and I get ready and head out the door to see Anthony.

I knock loudly at the door for a minute before I hear footsteps coming to answer it. As he opens the door, I see the most incredible sight I have ever seen. He stands there muscles bulging with no shirt on and his mesh shorts hanging dangerously low on his hips. I think he has a 12 pack not a 6 pack. I stare shamelessly at him with my mouth open, until his voice snaps me back to reality.

"Kendall, is everything ok?" He asks.

"Ummm...yes sorry. I came over here because there is something I wanted to talk to you about. Can I come in?" I ask.

He nods his head and we walk inside and he leads us up to his room. My memories from yesterday's events come flooding back to me and my face becomes flushed from embarrassment. He notices this and grabs my hands and pulls me down to sit next to him on the bed.

"Anthony, I came here to tell you..." before I can even get anything out he interrupts me.

"You aren't breaking things off with me are you? I mean I thought we had a good time together yesterday. I mean I had a really good time." He says with emphasis. I know he is referring to our little fool around session.

"What!? No I am not breaking up with you! I am actually trying to tell you that I broke things off with Jordan. I am choosing to be with you and only you." I tell him finally.

"What?" He asks his voice laced with shock.

"Yes, I actually called him a little while ago to tell..."

I start but don't get to finish as his lips crash into mine. His tongue grazes my bottom lip asking for entrance which I grant him and our kissing instantly becomes very heated. I break away for a moment to breathe and talk to him.

"Anthony, I care about you so much. I don't know why I am so drawn to you and why you make me feel the way you do, but you just do. I am falling hard for you. I just hope you don't break my heart." I tell him putting all my feelings out there and leaving myself vulnerable as hell.

I hope he doesn't break my heart.

"Kendall, you have no idea how I feel about you do you? Since the first time I laid eyes on you, I wanted you. You are the most beautiful girl in the world to me and you are smart and funny." He says to me.

He then kisses me urgently and I kiss him back with just as much passion. I suddenly remember that he is shirtless and I can't help but trace the lines of his muscles on his stomach as we kiss.

He groans, "Fuck Kendall. Do you know what you do to me?" He says.

God he is hot. We continue to kiss for a few moments, before we hear a gasp coming from the doorway of his bedroom.

Anthony is facing the door and looks up and yells, "Mom, what are you doing back so soon?" He looks at her panicked.

My face is red as a beet, but I know I have to face her sometime. It feels like my head goes in slow motion as I turn around to see her. What I was not prepared for was the person I saw when I turned around. I gasp as my eyes widen as wide as saucers and the words come out of my mouth in a whisper type shout..."Mrs. Tarantino?!"

Chapter 16- Anthony AKA Seth

K endall's POV

Shock. Compete and utter shock is what I am feeling right now. And major confusion. I feel like I have seen a ghost. Mrs. Tarantino looks back at me in complete shock as well. We are all speechless until realization sets in. Anthony is Seth. He has been Seth this whole time and he lied to me. I feel betrayed. I look to him with utter disgust.

"I can't believe you lied to me Anthony...or Seth.. whatever your real name is!! I trusted you and this is what you do?!" I scream in anger and rush out of the room.

"No!! He screams behind me. "Please don't leave,you have to listen to me." He pleads behind me.

I stop in my tracks and turn around to him.

"Why should I?! You have lied to me for 6 months about your identity! I was so broken hearted when you left me. You were my best friend. And all of the sudden one day you weren't there. I never even got to say good bye!!" I say as a tear streams down my cheek.

"You have no clue how badly I wanted to, but I couldn't." He starts to say but his mom cuts him off.

"Seth, don't say another word." She says firmly.

I look at her in disgust. She took him away from me and they lied the whole time we knew them. I have never felt so betrayed and angry before.

"I gave up having a relationship with Jordan for you and then I find this out. I can't even believe you." I say.

His mom interrupts the conversation again.

"Look, you are a sweet girl. You always have been Kendall. But there are things you have no clue about and can never know. Please leave and just forget about him. He will be leaving in just a few months and will be out of your life for good. We all will. But I beg of you not to tell anyone about any of this. If you do, you will be putting us all in very real danger." She says seriously with sadness in her eyes.

"Can someone just please tell me what is going on?" I ask looking into Seth's eyes.

I always get so lost in them. His mom and him exchange a look and I just know he won't tell me.

"I wish I could, but I can't Kendall. I am so sorry." He says holding his head down in shame.

"Fine. Don't call me, text me, or talk to me at school anymore. I want nothing to do with you." I lie to him.

I want everything to do with him. And this is breaking my heart in a million pieces.

"Goodbye." I say finally as I storm out of his front door and out of his life.

I go home and cry my eyes out. My mom asks me what is going on and I just tell her Anthony and I had a fight and broke up. I don't know if what his mom said about being in danger is true or not, but I don't want to find out. It's killing me not to tell my mom though that Anthony is Seth.

I go to school the next morning, and fill the girls in telling them the same story I told my mom. I hate all this lying and dishonesty. I keep passing Seth/Anthony in the hallway and I immediately look away, although I can feel his eyes stare at me like they are looking into my soul. I do my best to ignore him every chance I get. It's hard, but I have to.

The rest of the week goes by quickly, but I am still so bummed out. I don't have Jordan or Anthony anymore. Even though I may not have romantic feelings towards Jordan anymore, he was still my friend. I feel alone. I am glad I have my girl friends though. On Friday during lunch, the girls and I sit and talk about our plans for the weekend, when suddenly a guy walks up to our table. I recognize him from my history class. He asks me what I am doing this weekend. Wait, is he asking me out? I don't know if I am ready for that just yet. Just as I am about to tell him I am not interested, I hear an almost growl come from behind me. I turn around to see no one other than Anthony/Seth glaring at the poor boy talking to me.

"She's taken. Now get the fuck out of here." He seethes and the boy takes off running in the other direction.

Poor guy. Damn Anthony! I give him an angry look before saying,

"How dare you speak for me! I am not taken and you aren't my boss!" I yell but soon realize I am making a scene and I scurry off down the empty hallways.

Anthony follows behind me. As he catches up to me, he grabs my arm swings me around and with one swift movement he ushers me into a nearby empty classroom with the lights off. He cages me in against the wall. His close proximity is making me dizzy and my mind is thinking very dirty thoughts. Wait no. I can't think like that anymore.

"Kendall." He says hungrily.

"You are mine and only mine. You drive me wild and no one else can have you." He says as he attacks my lips.

It feels so amazing I can't help but kiss him back. I run my hands through his beautiful hair and he groans into the kiss. Man I don't want this to ever end. I feel drunk on him. I don't think I can let him go. He stops suddenly to finish his thoughts.

"No one can make you feel like this. Or kiss you here...." He says as he kisses down my neck.

I moan and he smirks pulling his face impossibly close to mine. "..or touch you." He says as he takes his hand and brushes it lightly down my arm and he snakes it back around my back pulling me even closer if that is possible. He finally stops at my ass which he squeezes delightfully and I hum in response.

He gives me one last chaste kiss and we hear the bell ring signaling lunch period is over.

"Meet me after school in our usual spot. I will tell you everything." He whispers as he walks out of the classroom suddenly.

I am left with my head reeling at what just happened and an ache between my legs. Damn him!!

Chapter 17- The Cat's Out Of The Bag

Anthony/Seth's POV

I can't stand it anymore. I have to tell her. I don't care what my mom says or thinks. I can't live without Kendall. I hate that she doesn't know the biggest secret in my life that I have been keeping since childhood and I was old enough to understand what was going on. I will feel so relieved to tell my best friend. After school, I head to our spot and am excited to see she listened to me and is waiting for me.

"This better be good." She says with her arms crossed. God she is so hot.

"First of all, we are going to go for a walk up the trail here. No one can hear us talking got it?" I tell her.

She nods her head yes and we begin walking.

"Listen, you aren't going to reveal to me that you are an axe murderer or something and then slit my throat are you?" She asks chuckling nervously.

"Really?" I ask her giving her knowing look.

"Ok so what is it?" She asks.

I fumble my hands around nervously for a moment before finding the courage to talk.

"So, first things first...my name really is Seth Tarantino. My father is Justin Tarantino. All of my life we told people he was a traveling businessman or in the military when in fact he does none of those things." I tell her as she looks at me skeptically.

"He works for the CIA. He is a spy and he has helped take down a lot of criminals in his lifetime all around the world. He always kept a low profile because he had to so no one knew who he was or what he did. But one day things went haywire while he was doing a job, and he got caught. Some Russian bad guys figured out who he was and they beat the crap out of him. He was battered within an inch of his life. They left him for dead. Then they started researching him and they found out where we lived. I am not sure how since everything is top secret in the government. They planned to come and kill my mom and I too for revenge. But my father was smart and had a personal body guard that helped keep a watch out for us. The body guard found out what they did to my dad and came and made us pack everything up and leave one night in the middle of the night. He told us we had to leave our old life behind and go into the witness protection program." I tell her as I feel like a weight has been lifted from me.

I finally told her the truth.

"Oh my God! That's why that day I woke up and found you gone, your house was a wreck." She remembers.

"Yes, shortly after we escaped they came and ransacked our house looking for us and looking for clues as to where we might be. But they never found us luckily. We can never let them know where we are. These people are bad news and even though it's been several years, they vowed to not rest until they killed our whole family." I tell her shakily.

She reaches out and grabs my hand and it instantly calms me down as she runs circles around the back of it and interlocks our fingers.

"They believe my father is dead. We haven't even seen him in 6 years. He's been in hiding since that day. We talk once a month briefly. It's been really hard on all of us especially mom. It's like they are divorced, but they are not. She misses him and I do too." I tell her honestly.

"I am so glad you told me. You have no idea how much I blamed myself. I thought you guys hated me and left because I got on your nerves or something." She says as I chuckle.

"I know that sounds ridiculous, remember I was only 10 at the time?!" She finishes as she begins to laugh lightly.

"Kendall, you have to promise me that you won't tell a soul. You can't slip up and call me Seth around anyone. No one can find out or we are as good as dead." I tell her solemnly.

"And by the way I am so sorry about your dad. I wanted to tell you that when you told me so bad, but I knew you would figure it out. He was a good man. Our parents were good friends. Our world just fell apart all because of my dad's job. I wonder how things would have turned out if all of this hadn't happened and we didn't leave?" I ask her.

"It would have ended up with the same result as far as us.." she points between us before leaning up and grabbing my face to kiss me fiercely, but softly. She drives me so wild. I grab her butt and pull her legs up so I can hold her in my arms and hug her close to me. We stop to take a breath and rest our foreheads together.

"But fate has destined us to be together no matter what apparently." I tell her honestly.

She smiles back at me nodding in agreeance. This girl means the world to me and I hope and pray she will keep my secret.

Chapter 18- Best Night Of My Life

K endall's POV

I am so glad I finally know the whole truth. Anthony really is Seth. It's so weird. But I am just happy that we are back together. The past week was one from complete hell. I hated being broken up with him. We decide to go out onto a date to celebrate our making up. My mom and Julie and Sarah were happy to hear we made up. Julie and Sarah both have boyfriends now as well so we can plan to go out on dates together and we can gossip about how our dates went when we go out alone. Seth's mom obviously doesn't know though and we have to be careful that she doesn't find out.

I dress in a pretty sundress that is a little shorter than I like to wear but it's really cute and looks good on me. I hear the doorbell ring and head downstairs to see my beautiful boyfriend smiling at me wearing a shirt that clings to him ever so nicely and jeans that look that they were made specifically for him. God is it hot in here?? He sees me check him out and smirks. Terd. He knows what he does to me. He looks at me too and I blush profusely. My mom tells us to have fun and we head to his car. Before we can get in, he grabs my arm and whips me around quickly putting his body in between my legs as he presses me up against the side of his car and cages me between his arms.

"This dress is making me want to not go anywhere and just tear it off of you and do things to you that would drive you insane." He says huskily.

I attempt to squeeze my legs together at the sensation he is giving me, but remember his body is between them. It feels like we were made for each other. Like two perfect puzzle pieces that fit together. He knows that I am getting aroused and he curses before smashing his lips against mine. My tongue begs his bottom lip for entrance which he allows as he moans into the kiss loudly.

"Fuck me." He says. I just smirk at him.

"Let's go before I take you against the side of my car out here in front of God and everyone." He says.

I can't ignore the pool forming between my folds now. I just half chuckle, half whimper against him as he removes himself from his previous position and I find myself yearning for him to touch me again. I can't ignore the overwhelming urge I have to constantly hold him or touch him or kiss him.

Seth decides to take me to a place just inside the city. We know we can't let his mom see us together, so we make the 1 hr drive to the city. He takes me to a beautiful little restaurant that has a breathtaking view of the skylines as it is in the upper level of a building. We look out onto the city as we talk and laugh. I can't stop smiling at him and he asks why.

"Because I never thought in a million years that you would be my boyfriend." I tell him honestly.

He thinks for a moment before answering,

"I have been in love with you since we were kids playing in the yard together. I almost kissed you I don't know how many times. You were beautiful then and you are beautiful now and I love hearing you call me your boyfriend. It's like a dream come true." He tells me as he kisses my hand.

Aww. That was so sweet. He admitted to me that he loved me. While that thought makes me nervous it also just feels right. Not like when Jordan said it to me before. And to be honest I think I love him too.

"I love you too. Honestly I think I always have. The feelings you give me when you kiss me or when I look at you. If that isn't love, I don't know what is." I tell him.

He squeezes my hand at my declaration. We finish our meal and head back out towards home.

On the way back he says, "There is a place I want to show you. Can I take you?" He asks and I nod my head yes.

He takes a few turns onto some back roads. He drives us up a steep incline on a dirt road. It seems to go on forever. Once we reach the top he stops and parks the car. I look out to see that we are overlooking all of Arlington Heights.

"I think this view is better than the city." He tells me.

I look over at him and he looks absolutely beautiful. I can't help myself when I lean over and kiss him hard.

"You wanna star gaze with me for a bit?" He asks as he breaks the kiss.

"Sure." I tell him. He grabs a blanket from his trunk and lays it on the ground. He lies down and I lay next to him placing my head on top of his outstretched arm that is draped around my back. He starts to draw circles on my arm and then he runs his hand back and forth along my back and side. This simple gesture ignites a fire in me. I turn over and kiss him as hard as I ever have, not even stopping to take a breath. He is the first to pull away as he looks at me hungrily with puffy lips from my assault just a few minutes ago.

"Kendall, I love you and don't want you to do anything you are not ready for yet. But when you kiss me like that, it's really hard to control myself." He says strained.

I look down and notice how hard he is for me. That just turned me on even more. I answer him by kissing him just as passionately as I did before and he grabs me and rolls me on top of him not breaking the kiss once. I decide to break the kiss only to lean up and begin to slowly strip my dress off. I am left in nothing but my underwear. I didn't wear a bra. His eyes grow dark with lust.

"Kendall! What are you doing?" He asks me.

"What do you think I am doing?" I reply.

"Kendall. I don't want you to feel like you have to do this." He says concerned.

"I have never wanted anything more in my entire life. I know it seems like we have only known each other a few months but we have really know each other our whole lives. We are soul mates and there is no one else I want to lose my virginity to than you. You are it for me. I love you Seth." I tell him honestly.

That's all it takes to convince him as he pulls me down on top of him and my bare breasts touch his clothed chest. We kiss passionately as he runs his hands through my hair and down my naked back. I moan and he quickly flips us over so that he is now towering over me looking down on me hungrily. Fuck that's a turn on. He looks to my breasts and suddenly I feel a little self conscious.

As if he can sense my worry, he says, "You are absolutely perfect."

Then he begins to suck my nipple slowly and deliberately driving me insane with need. He makes me throb in my core. I moan and groan loudly in pleasure. He then starts to kiss down my stomach, making his way to my treasured place. Oh God. So Jordan tried this once and I remember we had to stop because I laughed so hard at how bad it tickled me. I hurt his feelings so bad and I felt terrible. I hope that doesn't happen again. He reaches my entrance and slowly and seductively removes my underwear. Now I am completely naked in front of him. But before I can feel self conscious again, he begins to lick my folds like it was his favorite meal and I scream and moan out in pleasure. This doesn't tickle. It feels amazing. Poor Jordan had no idea what he was doing. I feel myself building again like I did when he fingered me. I know what's about to happen.

"Seth! I am cumming!" I scream out as he continues his attack with his tongue until my high has been completely ridden out.

I lay there dazed for a moment as I notice he has begun to strip. And God I like what I see. Now it's my turn to look at him lustfully. I knew he was big from when I jacked him off, but oh God now that I see it I wonder if it's going to fit inside me? He climbs back on top of me and kisses me slowly and seductively. Making me yearn for him.

"Baby, I need you." I moan out.

He looks me in the eyes and searches back and forth between them. I guess silently asking for permission. I nod yes and begin kissing him again.

"This is going to hurt for a moment but it will feel better as I move and will get less painful each time we do it." He tells me honestly.

I again shake my head in understanding. I feel him line up at my entrance and slide into me slowly filling me completely. Like two pieces to the same puzzle, it fits perfectly. It was a little painful at first put as he picks up his pace it starts to feel absolutely wonderful.

"Fuck Kendall. You feel so amazing." He moans out.

I just moan and groan incoherently. I feel myself build and I know I am about to go again.

I whimper out "Seth yes!! Right there. Oh God!" As I cum for the second time tonight.

"Fuck I love to hear you moan my name like that. My real name. It's such a fucking turn on. You are mine. Remember that?" He says as he slows his pace for a few moments and looks at me fiercely.

"Yours." I pant out breathlessly. With a few more fast pumps in and out he finds his release moaning my name in the process.

We lay there in sated bliss for a while with the blanket wrapped around us. We are actually rolled up in it like a burrito. We rub each other's skin as we look up at the stars.

"This has been the best night of my life. And even though I didn't think I could fall in love with you anymore, I just did." He says heartfeltedly.

"I love you." I tell him simply.

"I love you and will never love anyone else. You are it for me." He tells me.

I kiss him so slow and soft.

"Kendall, we have to stop or I will stay here and fuck you all night long." He says.

I kind of chuckle but when he doesn't laugh I know he is serious. I get up and we start to get dressed. He takes me home and I know now we will be together forever. I love him an impossibly insane amount and I can't wait to do what we did tonight again.

Chapter 19- Crazy Ride Home

Kendall's POV

I wake up feeling wonderful. Is that what sex does to you? Makes you in a good mood. I mean it felt wonderful. I can't wait to do it again. I go to get out of bed but soon feel why people complain that your first time hurts. I am really sore down there. Maybe I am not ready just yet. I have to walk very slowly to get into the shower to get myself cleaned up and ready for the day.

Even though I still have to walk slowly, my ache starts to ease some. I get to school and see Seth standing at the lockers waiting for me smiling. He sees me moving slowly and frowns.

I reach him and he bends down and whispers in my ear, "Is that from what I did?" He asks concerned.

"Last time I checked, it was mutual. I wanted it just as bad as you did." I whisper back to him.

He smiles but says "I didn't mean to hurt you though." He says sadly.

I grab his face so he looks me in the eyes. "You didn't hurt me. It's just sore. Like when you work out and your muscles get sore." I explain to him.

He just nods and I kiss his lips softly.

"So I actually need to tell you something and you may kill me." He says fearfully. I look at him annoyed and ask him what it is.

"I didn't use any protection last night. I kind of got carried away in the moment and wasn't thinking straight." He says nervously.

"Well I have been on birth control for a year now anyway or trust me I would have stopped you.I My mom made me get on it when she caught me and Jordan making out one time." I chuckle at the memory and Seth scowls at the mention of Jordan's name.

"Sorry. Didn't mean to bring that up." I apologize.

"Just remember you are mine." He whispers huskily into my ear tickling my neck with his breath.

It sends a wonderful sensation through me as I close my eyes. I open my eyes to see he has left me. What a terd! Got me all worked up for nothing.

I go to class and my day goes by smoothly. Well until the end of the day. As I leave my last class to look for Seth, I find him in a compromising position with his ex Cassie. She has her body pressed up against his as he looks pinned by her against his locker. I walk up to them as fast as I can and can't control my myself as I pull her from his body as hard as I can and she goes flying back across the hallway.

"What the fuck you bitch!?" She yells in my face.

"No you look bitch. Stay the fuck away from my man. He broke up with you and has moved on. You need to too." I yell back at her.

I don't know what has come over me. I have never felt this angry before. She just scoffs and walks off knowing she isn't going to win this battle.

"That was fucking hot." Seth comes up behind me whispering in my ear.

I turn around quickly glaring at him and his expression changes quickly.

"Why the hell were you letting her do that?! You weren't even trying to fight back. You still want her don't you?" I ask him feeling insecure.

"What?! No! I can't stand her. She literally had just pushed herself up on me when you came up. I didn't even have time to react before you did!" He says in defense.

"Yeah whatever." I say as I turn around and storm off and out of the school building as he follows me out.

"Wait, are you jealous?" He asks.

"Jealous. Ha! Someone thinks very highly of himself doesn't he?" I say in a scoff.

"Yeah ok whatever." He says.

We both walk to his car and get inside. He drives us both in silence until we get to a turn off down a deserted road and he pulls over.

"Look Kendall, I am sorry. I just couldn't help...." He starts but I stop him by jumping in his lap and kissing him as passionately as I can.

I force my tongue in his mouth and I stroke him through his pants. I unzip and unleash his throbbing cock. I slide off my underwear quickly as I wore a skirt to school today and I slide myself onto him in one swift motion.

"Kendall what are you doing...?" He starts to ask but I start to bounce up and down on his cock quickly as I kiss him. After his initial protest, he kisses me back with just as much intensity as I speed up my pace, going up and then slamming back hard down onto his huge member. After only a few minutes I am screaming his name as I cum everywhere and he finds his release at the same time as me.

"What the hell was that?" He asks me breathlessly.

I just look him at him intensely as I stare over his beautiful features.

"You're mine." I tell him possessively.

"Yes baby. All yours. I promise." He says before kissing me softly for a moment.

I then climb off of him and back into my seat. I put my underwear back on as he zips himself back up. He backs up and we head quietly back down the road.

"Ok...so maybe I am a little jealous." I say as he smirks at me.

"You are something else." He says as he shakes his head and grabs my hand and holds it in his.

Chapter 20- The Disappearance

Kendall's POV

"Yes! Yes! Oh God yes!" I scream as Seth pounds into me. Of course my mom isn't home. We barely made it in the door from school and he grabbed me and is now pounding into me as I yell out in pleasure.

"Kendall. Baby. I love you so much. You are so fucking hot. You turn me on so bad." He says to me as he slams into me.

As soon as he is done with his declaration I come undone "Seth I am cumming baby!" I yell and he finds his release soon after.

God. We are both so horny. What is wrong with us? One day he jumps my bones and the next I am jumping his. We just lose all control around each other. It's like we need to feel that closeness. That bond we have is so strong and we need to show each other all the time how much we love each other. We have had sex pretty much every day for the last month. We just literally can't keep our hands off of each other. Imagine if Seth had never left and we got together sooner? Lord knows how many times we would have done it by now. I just won't ever get enough of his touch.

I have done very well to keep Seth/Anthony's secret. I call him Anthony or honey or some type of term of endearment when at school and usually Seth when we are in private. Especially during sex. His mom still has no clue he went behind her back and told me everything. She doesn't even know we are still dating. I hate lying to her and I hate that Seth has to lie to her. She thinks he spends all his time with his buddies or at baseball practice/games. In one month, Seth will graduate and it's killing me. I know he is leaving again and I don't think I can take that again. The realization hits me and I find myself crying.

"Baby, what it wrong?" He asks me as he pets my face.

"I just realized that in one month you will graduate and you are going to leave me again. I don't think I can take it. The first time about killed me and I am sure this next time will. Especially after all we have shared together." I tell him truthfully.

"Kendall, about that. I am not leaving you. I am going to stay here and go to college until you graduate and then I will go with you wherever you go. I am not losing you again." He says to me lovingly.

I kiss him and hug him to me excitedly.

"But what about your plans and what about your mom?" I ask.

"Well after graduation, I plan to tell mom that you know our secret and how long you have known and how you have kept my secret this long. That will prove to her that you are loyal and won't tell anyone. Then we can be together." He says.

"I love you so much Seth." I tell him.

"I love you too baby." He says as he kisses me.

Life is so perfect.

Until it wasn't.

A week later we are sitting around at lunch talking about our prom plans and graduation and Seth gets called up to the office. That's weird. He looks at me confused but shakes it off and walks up to the office. We all just assumed it was the guidance counselor talking about upcoming graduation. They have been pulling seniors out of class to discuss things lately. I can't believe he graduates in just a few short weeks!! As lunch comes to an end and Seth still hasn't returned, I go looking for him in the office. It's weird that it's taking this long. I walk into the office and ask if he is still in there and they tell me he left 20 mins ago.

"What? With who?" I ask.

That's not like him to leave and not even text me. He usually gives me a ride home. I can't hide the sense of uneasiness I feel and the next few words only make me feel even worse.

"His dad picked him up." They tell me.

Oh my God. That can't be good. I try to act casual about it but I turn away and go out into the hall feeling sick. I hope he is ok. I try to text him but I don't get a response. Another suspicious thing. At the end of the day there is still no sign of him and no response to my texts. I go to his locker to take a peek inside. I have his combo memorized because he always tells me to go get one of his hoodies out of it when I am cold. I open the locker and see his book bag along with his phone still in there untouched. This just reassures me that I was right. Seth's in trouble. I have to find him.

Chapter 21- Something Is Wrong

Kendall's POV

I immediately leave the school building and know the first place I have to go. I have to go see if his mom is still home and ok. I go there and see her car is still in the driveway. I peek inside and it seems to be untouched. I knock on the door and she answers quickly.

"What are you doing here?" She asks rudely.

I don't take it personally. I know why she is always on edge.

"Listen, I know you hate me and you don't trust me but Anthony was taken from school today by someone claiming to be his father and he left all his things at school. Something is very wrong." I tell her on the brink of tears.

She instantly breaks down and I have to scoop her up in my arms and bring her back inside so she doesn't bring attention to us. Who knows who is watching? I shake that creepy feeling off and do my best to hold it together while his mom is falling apart.

"Oh God they took him!! They took my baby!!" She screams and cries.

"Listen, everything is going to be ok. We are going to find him. I won't rest until we do." I tell her honestly.

I will be damned if I let someone take him away from me.

"Why do you care?! I thought you hated him?" She says.

I am not going to let her know that I know everything yet.

"I could never hate him. He was my best friend and he still is. I lost him once and I will NOT lose him again!" I say determined.

She smiles at me through her tears. "What do we do next?" She asks me.

"I think we have to wait to see if he contacts us. I am not sure who took him or what they want but they are messing with the wrong people." I tell her.

We sit there trying to make conversation waiting to hear something from Seth. Suddenly her phone rings startling us both. It's from a blocked number.

"Baby is that you?" She answers hysterically and puts it on speaker phone.

"Yeah mom. They made me call you. They have been watching us for a year. They have known where we were since then." He tells her.

Suddenly a voice with a strong Russian accent gets on the phone.

"Listen, we know where you are. We have known for a while but we are not worried about you. We know your husband is still alive. But they are hiding him a little too well. We kept thinking he would slip up eventually and come to see you but he never does. Give us his location." They demand.

I look at Seth's mom and I can tell she is freaking out internally.

"I don't know his location. He has never told us." She says shakily.

"Liar!!!" They scream.

"No, no I swear they won't tell us. I haven't seen him in 6 years. I thought he was dead too." She says crying.

"Listen here bitch. You find out his location by noon tomorrow or I slit your son's throat."

We both gasp at that and the water works start as the guy hangs up.

"No! No! Seth!!" I scream but it's no use.

We both cry hysterically for several minutes. I try to pull myself together. I need to think clearly. I text my mom telling her I am staying at Julie's house tonight. I need to be here for Seth's mom and to help think of a plan. Then I start asking Mrs. Tarantino questions.

"Can you get ahold of Mr. Tarantino?" I ask her.

"No, he calls from an unidentifiable phone number once a month. He tried not to make anything look suspicious. We have moved all around the country trying to escape these men but we always would get information from the Feds that they were tracking us again. These men are good. Every time they think they have caught them and try to bust them they come up empty handed." She tells me.

"Is there another government official that you can contact?" She looks at me suspiciously. I am sure she is wondering how I knew anything but now is not the time. Then all of the sudden it's like a light bulb went off.

"I know who I can call that will get ahold of him." She says as she starts looking through her phone frantically for the number.

She talks to the person on the other end of the phone explaining the situation. Within a few minutes she is getting a phone call.

"Justin, oh God they have our boy!!" She cries hysterically.

"I don't want to give them your location but I have to save our son!" She says frantic.

"Denise I know. I am going to text you my address. This is my real address please give it to them. I am going to let them take me. I can't do this anymore. I am tired of running and tired of putting you in danger. I love you and will always love you. Tell Seth I love him too." He says solemnly.

Mrs. Tarantino sobs uncontrollably for a few moments before telling him she loves him too and hanging up with him. A few seconds go by and the phone dings with the address. Huh. He is in Texas. No wonder Seth wanted to go there after graduation. He wanted to be closer to his dad. They knew which state he was in even if they didn't know the exact location. So now we have to sit here and wait for the phone to ring so we can tell them.

We stay up talking all night knowing we both can't possibly sleep. I admit to her that Seth told me everything and she figured it was a matter of time before he did. But she also knows that it wasn't anything that we did that led them to us. She tells me more about what his father did to these Russians to piss them off so badly, now that the cat is out of the bag. He apparently got some Russian leader in a lot of trouble and he was put in prison for life. Some of his supporters and people that worked with him are the ones that have been seeking revenge on Mr. Tarantino.

"They aren't going to rest until he is in prison or dead. They left him thinking he was dead once. Now they are going to make sure they finish the job." She says as she sobs. I do my best to console her.

"Thank you Kendall. I am so sorry I treated you badly and didn't think we could trust you. I was wrong. I don't know what I would have done if you weren't here with me." She says.

I just smile back at her and tell her "it's been my pleasure."

At some point we must have nodded off while sitting at the kitchen table because we wake with a startle as the phone rings loudly in our ears. Mrs. Tarantino answers it quickly and puts it on speakerphone. Before she even has a chance to say anything they ask, "Do you have the address?" They ask gruffly.

"Yes. It's 13789 10th Avenue, Galveston, TX 77550." She says shakily.

"Smart lady. Tell him that he had better not try to pull anything funny like have the Feds ready to pick us up. He had better be alone. Once we figure out he is alone, we will let the boy go." The man says cryptically.

"Wait. That's not what you said..." she tries to say but he hangs up.

"Oh God, what if they lied and they kill them both!!" She screams and cries.

"Stop. Don't think that way." I tell her.

"Please call your contact and have them let your husband know not to have anyone there to try to intercept the men. We have to hope and pray that they both make it out ok. We can't give up yet." I tell her desperately trying to believe my own words.

She does as I say and calls her contact to let Mr. Tarantino know that he needs to be completely alone so they will let Seth go.

"What now?" She asks me.

"We just sit and wait until we hear something." I tell her. "That's all we can do."

Chapter 22- The Kidnapping

Seth AKA "Anthony" POV

I can't believe this! These bastards found us after all these years and think they are going to take me away from my girl. That's not happening. I don't care what has to happen but they won't succeed. I hope my dad has a plan in place. They have beaten me and choked me trying to get me to talk. I honestly never knew dad's exact location. He wouldn't tell us. He didn't know our last either. Everything had to be top secret. I am honestly so sick of all of it. I can't believe they were so brazen to come in my school and pretend to be my dad.

Flashback to the day I was taken....

"Anthony Taylor, please come to the office." We hear the secretary call from the office. Kendall and I just look at each other in confusion before I head to the office. If I had known that might be the last moment I would see my girl, I would have kissed her like my life depended on it. I reach the office and I see a man dressed in a suit with dark slicked back hair. He kind of resembles my dad from behind. Same hair, same build. When he turns around I realize it is not my dad.

"Son!" He says faking excitement.

Fuck. Who is this guy and what is he doing? He gives me a look that only I can see. It tells me not to fuck around and to just go with it.

"Hey." I say faking a smile.

"I need you to come with me. Your grandfather isn't doing well. He is in the hospital." He lies.

I just nod my head and follow. After we have left the building he pulls a gun out.

"You will do everything I say or I will kill you, your mom, and your little girlfriend." He says.

Fuck.

My heart breaks at the thought of them hurting my family. I just nod my head in understanding. I won't let that happen. I will die before I let them.

We get into the strangers car, he handcuffs me and he calls a man and they are speaking Russian. The guy that picked me up from school didn't have an accent though. I wonder how he was able to mask that. They would have seen through it then.

"How did you get them to believe that you were my dad?" I ask skeptically.

"Your school really needs a better system. I came in there and showed them a fake ID. I had a concealed weapon. They had no idea." He says chuckling.

"Why don't you have an accent?" I ask intrigued.

"I took English classes and learned how to mask it." He says.

We spend the rest of the ride in silence. We drive until we end up in the city. We stop outside what looks like an old abandoned building. He parks the car and we head inside. He ties me up to a chair and then a group of men surround me all speaking Russian. One of them starts speaking English to me but he has a very strong Russian accent.

"Where the fuck is your father?" He asks me.

"No fucking clue. I thought he was dead." I lie.

Pow!! I get slapped with a deadly force and I instantly feel blood trickle down my cheek. Fuck that hurt. I don't flinch though.

"Don't lie to me!!" He booms.

"I am not. I don't know where he is. We haven't seen or heard from him in many years." I tell him.

He gets in my face spitting as he talks. "If you are lying to me. I will cut every appendage from your body starting with your ears and dance on top of the carnage as I watch you bleed out. Don't fuck with me." He says dangerously.

I try to pretend I am not scared, but inside I am shaking.

"I'm not. Let me call my mom and you can ask her. She will tell you the same thing." I tell him.

Mom and I were always instructed to act like he was dead and that we didn't know he was alive. He stares at me and I stare back stone cold serious. Not giving him any hint that I am lying.

"Give me a phone!" He demands his men and he asks for her number which I give him.

He puts it on speakerphone. It rings only once before I hear my mom's frantic voice. Thank God she is ok.

"Baby is that you?" She asks.

"Yeah mom. They have known where we are for a year." I tell her honestly.

The Russian guy with the thick accent interrupts. "Listen, we know where you are. We have known for a while now but are not worried about you. We know your husband is still alive. They are hiding him a little too well. We kept thinking he would slip up and come see you but he never did. Tell us his location." He says to her.

"I don't know his location. He has never told us." She tells him.

"Liar!!" He booms angrily.

"No, no I swear! We haven't seen him in 6 years! We thought he was dead." She lies.

Thank God she told him the same thing I did. I breath in relief.

"Listen here bitch! You find his location by noon tomorrow or I slit your son's throat!!" He yells hanging up the phone.

Well I guess this is my time to go. He looks at me evilly before coming over and punching me hard several times in the face and then pulling his knife to my throat.

"I will take pleasure in doing this tomorrow if your precious mom doesn't come through." He seethes.

I just swallow hard praying silently that I make it through some how. I have to make it back to my momma and my girl.

End of flashback...

It's now 2 days later. I sit here dirty, tired, beaten and sore, and starving. They all left me here yesterday after finding out my dad's location. I can't help but hope and pray that I am found before they get back. I know they lied. They have every intention of killing me and not letting me go. But what if they all get killed and don't come back for me? I will die here if no one finds me. I begin to feel very weak and dehydrated.

Please God let someone find me.

As if he answers my prayer, I hear a door open and a strange man comes stalking in. Is he another one?

"Oh my God! What the hell is going on here?" He screams.

Thank God. He's not one.

"Help me!" I scream a pitiful scream as I have hardly any energy.

The man runs over and unties me.

"We have to get out of here before they come back." I tell him urgently.

He nods his head in understanding and he helps me up as I hold onto him and we leave the building. He puts me in his car and we drive away as quickly as possible.

Chapter 23- It's All Over Finally

Seth's POV

We speed down the road and the man starts asking questions.

"What were you doing there?" He asks.

"I was kidnapped. They left yesterday and haven't returned. You just saved my life. I would have died had I stayed in there another day." I tell him breathlessly.

"Why did you come in there?" I ask him.

"Well I am a real estate agent and someone was interested in buying that piece of property to renovate. I came to check things out before they came to meet me." He tells me.

I groan a little bit in pain.

"I am going to stop to get you something to eat and drink." He says.

"That's fine. But please make it a drive thru. I need to get home to my girl. She's probably worried sick." I tell him.

He smiles knowingly and nods his head as we pull into a McDonald's.

Kendall's POV

I haven't hardly slept since Friday night when we got the call from Seth. Yesterday we gave them his father's location and we haven't heard a word since from anybody. We are both sick with worry but I haven't left Seth's mom's sight. It's now Sunday afternoon and I am trying to hold it together for her. But if we don't hear something soon, I am going to have to go home. My mom isn't going to let me stay over at anyone's house even if she thinks I am still at a friends house on a school night. I try to make small talk with her but it's so hard to keep our brains distracted from our overbearing thoughts. Neither of us have eaten, so I make us some grilled cheese sandwiches and I try to get her to eat with me. We both pick at our food while our frantic thoughts consume us.

Seth's POV

My rescuer is nice enough to drive me all the way home. I offer to pay him money for his troubles but he refuses. As we pull into the driveway, another strange car pulls in just ahead of us and I tense in fear that it's the Russian men that kidnapped me. Once I see who gets out though, a sense of overwhelming relief hits me as well as a feeling of euphoria. I see my father standing there looking back at the vehicle I pulled up in. I step out quickly showing him it's me. He originally tenses and even goes to reach for his firearm before realizing it's me. We give each other a bear hug as we breathe sighs of relief for probably the first time in the last 48 hrs.

"It's all over son." He says to me and I lose it in his embrace.

My savior steps out of his car and I introduce him to my father and ask him to please come inside with us. My dad and I walk up to the door with our arms locked around each other with my guardian angel in tow behind us. We ring the doorbell and pause while we wait for the them to open the door. It's a matter of seconds before my mom swings the door open and embraces us both in hugs as she kisses my cheeks repeatedly and then grabs my father holding him close to her kissing him like her life depended on it. Normally that would gross me out but with the circumstances being what they are, I don't even care. I am glad they are happy. I look away from them to see my beautiful girl staring back at me with tears in her eyes and a completely grief stricken face. I run to her and pick her up into my arms hugging her and kissing her like never before.

"I thought I would never see you again!" She sobs.

"I will always come back to you. I love you so much." I tell her.

And I do. She is everything to me. I kiss her passionately until we hear my parents clear their throats behind us and we stop our mini make out session to look at them.

"Kendall?!" My dad says clearly in shock at who he is seeing.

"Yes Mr. Tarantino. It's so good to see you again." She says. She is so amazing and beautiful.

We all sit down together and I introduce them to my savior and everyone thanks him repeatedly for rescuing me. Then dad tells us the story of what happened. Apparently the Russians came to him but were still too stupid to get him. They came in and shot him repeatedly in the chest before running from the house and attempting to flee. Of course dad was wearing a bulletproof vest and was fine. He isn't dumb. If they hadn't gone for the chest though it might have been a different story. The Feds caught up to them at the airport and arrested all of them and gave them a fake plea deal to get them to rat each other out. It worked and they gained enough evidence to put all of them away for life. They also get intel on some other Russian guys that they are on their way to surprise and bust. Dad tells us he has retired and is done. Now that all of this is over, he just wants to be home with his family for the remainders of his years. My mom is beyond happy and relieved to hear all this. This is probably the happiest I have seen her in years. She tells us about how much Kendall helped her to get through this and that she was smart enough to realize something was wrong right away. That's my girl. I have honestly never felt as relieved as I am right now. My mind is at peace for the first time in years. Everything is perfect.

Chapter 24- Destined To Be Together

Seth's POV

That night, Kendall and I can't stand the thought of being apart and my parents get it. Plus I think they need some alone time too as gross as that is. But we decide to tell Kendall's mom that my mom had a last minute trip out of town and that I really didn't want to stay alone. She told us it was fine but I had to sleep on the couch. Well so she thinks...

After her mom goes to sleep, I sneak up into her room and she acts so surprised that I am in there.

"I wasn't going to stay down there and not cuddle with my baby." I tell her honestly.

"Well you will have to go back down before she gets up in the morning." She says.

"Deal." I say as I strip down to my boxers and climb under the sheets with her.

She is wearing a very silky night gown and I can see her hardened nipples underneath it as she wears no bra. Fuck she turns me on. I groan in excitement at the sight of her and she shakes her head.

"We can't do anything. You just went through a traumatic experience. Look at the cuts and bruises you got." She says as she traces over gently where they hit me.

"Can you kiss them for me and make them better?" I ask her with a pouty lip.

She giggles and says "I guess."

Yeah like she doesn't want to. She looks at me with lust just as much as I do her. She begins to kiss where every cut scratch and bruise is on my body. She starts with my face and then moves down to my neck and stomach and she stops just above my throbbing cock. She can tell she has excited me and she begins to rub me a bit. And then she takes me completely by surprise as she pulls my dick out and begins to suck it slowly and sensually.

"Kendall. Fuck that feels so good baby." I moan quietly so I don't wake up her mom.

She just hums in response as she picks up her pace. She alternates stroking it with her hand and sucking it. I know it's too much to take at once in her mouth.

Not that I am bragging or anything.

She continues her assault on me until I am a moaning mess and cum all over inside of her mouth.

"Holy fuck baby. That felt amazing." I tell her honestly.

She smiles back at me as she lays her head next to mine. Now I need her even more. I capture her lips quickly devouring every inch of her mouth with my tongue and lips. She groans underneath me and I can feel her hard buds beneath my bare chest. I reach up and rub them giving them a soft twist in between my fingers. I then gradually move my hand down until I am under her nightgown and...fuck. She isn't wearing any underwear. God damn she's hot. She looks at me innocently breaking the kiss.

"What? I don't like sleeping in any undergarments." She explains.

Now she just really turned me on. I begin kissing her passionately as I stroke her beautiful folds with my fingers. "Oh...uh...yes..." she moans almost incoherently as I pick up my pace.

Before long she is thrashing beneath me trying not to be loud and holding back as her orgasm flows through her body.

"Man, I wish you could scream my name right now." I tell her huskily.

She just blushes and I kiss her again this time much more sweetly and softly as I push her nightgown up and pull it over her head only breaking the kiss to take it off all the way. I look at her beautiful body underneath of me and I almost get off just looking at her. She is so fucking beautiful. I continue to kiss her again as I line up at her entrance and push myself in between her legs. She welcomes me by wrapping her legs around my back and I thrust into her in one quick motion. She moans and groans as I fill her up and stretch her to capacity. She was made just for me. I fit perfectly in her. I pick up my pace as I pound into her. She arches her back up to meet me thrust for thrust. She is driving me wild. I begin to trail kisses down her neck and she moans quietly as we both get closer to our climax.

"Say my name baby. Please. I love it when you do. Tell me you are cumming." I say and almost at my command she has one of the best orgasms I have seen her have thus far and she whisper yells my name saying "Oh God yes Seth. You made me go everywhere." Her words are my undoing as well.

I lay there still buried inside her for a while as I kiss her and we pet each other, until I can't stand the tickling feeling any more and I roll over next to her. I wrap her up in my arms.

"Marry me." I tell her. She looks at me in utter shock.

"What? I am not talking about tomorrow or anything but I want you to marry me. You are mine and I am yours and I want you to have my last name. Plus I am insanely in love with you." I tell her sincerely.

She just looks up at me beaming. "Give me 3 years. Let me get through college and I will marry you. I promise." She tells me.

I kiss her lips and we both begin to fall asleep quickly, completely exhausted from this crazy weekend. Thank God I set my alarm on my phone to make sure I am up and out of her room before her mom wakes up in the morning. My last thoughts before falling asleep is how lucky I have been to have met my soulmate at 5 years old. I kiss her softly on her forehead knowing that I am finally safe after all these years and my soulmate has agreed she will marry me one day. I sleep probably one of the best nights of sleep of my life in her arms that night. Destined to be together for life. Fate always being in our favor.

Epilogue

Kendall's POV

5 years later...

I wake up feeling tired and nauseated for the 3rd time this week. What is wrong with me? I realize after a few moments that it's Thanksgiving Day and there is a lot that needs to be done. I jump out of bed and head downstairs to find my beautiful husband is up making us breakfast and he looks good enough to eat himself.

Stop. I need to focus.

There is so much to do today. I have to prepare several deserts before we head over to Seth's parents house for dinner tonight. My mom and her new husband are coming too.

My mother was shocked when we finally told her that "Anthony" really was Seth. We told her an abbreviated form of what happened leaving out that Seth was ever kidnapped. I don't ever want her to worry about me. All is safe now. Seth's dad really did retire and has been more involved in his family's life than ever. Seth and I got married 2 years ago during my senior year of college. It was a beautiful wedding with our close friends and family in attendance. My mom met her future husband there. Remember the real estate agent that rescued Seth? Well he's my step dad now. Seth always invited him to events during the years following his kidnapping. He made him part of the family. Fate really has really played a roll in so many things in our lives. Although I was a little hurt that she could move on from my dad, I realized that I didn't want her to spend the rest of her life alone. She doesn't deserve that. She deserves all the happiness in the world. And at least it was with the person responsible for saving my husband. Mom also doesn't know that part either. It's our little secret. She just thinks he's a close family friend of Seth's.

I sneak down the stairs and end up behind Seth completely undetected as I snake my arms around his waste from behind. He turns around and kisses me passionately, picking me up and placing me on top of the counter top so he can deepen the kiss. Before we get carried away I pull away.

"As much as I want to continue this, I really have a ton of stuff to get ready before heading to your parents house in a bit." I tell him honestly.

He looks at me with a pouty lip for a moment before realizing I am right and helping me down off the counter. Seth and I have an insatiable hunger for each other. Always have. Always will. Having sex never gets old and we have had it in just about every room in this house. His stamina levels are off the charts. We go to sit down and eat breakfast when the nausea I was feeling hits hard and I feel like I am going to vomit. I rush to the bathroom and empty the contents of my stomach. Ugh that was awful.

"Babe, oh God are you ok?"

Seth asks rushing up behind me. I just give him a "really" look and he gets quiet. He helps me up and I instantly get dizzy and he has to grab me to keep me from falling.

"Baby, you are sick and are going to lay down. We aren't going to dinner tonight." He says firmly.

"No baby please! I have worked so hard to plan all of this. We can't miss it. I will go back and rest for a bit I promise. It was probably something I ate yesterday." I tell him.

He looks at me skeptically for a moment before hesitantly agreeing with me as I head back to bed. I feel so exhausted it takes only seconds before I fall asleep.

I wake up a little while later unsure of the time. I feel a lot better. I suddenly feel a really bad urge to pee and I jump up and head to our ensuite quickly. As I relieve myself, my eyes focus in on the box of tampons on the shelf in front of me and I realize I haven't had my period yet this month. I am a few weeks late. We have been so busy with work and everything I just completely forgot. Then my mind has a scary, but exciting thought. Could I be pregnant? I mean we both agreed to officially start trying after the holidays were over but we haven't exactly been very careful recently. And we have been having sex a lot! I suddenly remember that I bought a pack of pregnancy tests about a month ago since we talked about starting to try for a baby. I quickly grab one before I finish going and I hold it under the stream. I leave it sitting on the counter as I pace around the room. It's a digital test so it's pretty foolproof. There is no trying to guess with the whole lines thing. The test says wait 3 minutes before reading the results. After time is up,'I look down to see the display with the word Pregnant lit up in the test window. Oh my God. I am going to be a mom. A tear trickles down my face out of happiness and I quickly decide I am going to tell everyone tonight at dinner, even Seth. I have to keep it a secret until then though.

tairs to start making my deserts and realize what time it is!! You it's 2:00! How could Seth let me sleep this long?! I go search for him to see him sitting on our back deck just enjoying life.

"Seth!! Why the hell did you let me sleep so long?!!!" I yell startling him.

"Calm down baby. I took care of everything. I made all the deserts and they are all cooling in the fridge. I even cleaned up all of my mess. I just wanted you to rest so you could feel better. How do you feel?" He asks concerned.

God he is so sweet. I let my emotions get the better of me. Must be the hormones. I start to cry and he looks at me concerned.

"God baby you aren't ok are you?" He asks worriedly.

"Yes I am. It's just you are so sweet." I say as I wrap my arms around him.

Fuck I want him right now. I begin kissing him passionately and undoing his belt.

"Baby what the hell?" He asks.

I just look at him like "are you really questioning me?" and he instantly shuts up and picks me up in his arms and carries me to our bedroom. We strip each other of our clothes quickly and we fuck hard and fast in our bed and it drives me wild.

"What was that for?" He asks me.

"I just wanted you right then and there." I tell him honestly.

Again I think my hormones took over.

"Well you can do that to me anytime." He tells me smirking.

We both clean up and get dressed and gather all the deserts and head over to his parents house.

We get there and all of our parents are already there having a good time. They have become such good friends again and it makes my heart happy. We sit and enjoy our dinner and before we have desert I tell them I have a surprise for everyone. I grab a small wrapped package from my purse and place it in front of Seth.

"This is an early Christmas present." I tell him and we all watch him smiling as he opens it up.

He unwraps the tissue paper and stares at the test wide eyed before picking it up from the box and saying "You're pregnant?!"

I nod my head yes smiling and he picks me up and holds me in his arms as he kisses me with so much love and adoration.

"We're going to be grandparents!!" Our parents all yell excitedly around us.

We all hug each other and start talking baby names and all that. Seth holds me to him on the couch after dinner petting my belly.

"I can't believe you have our baby growing in there."' He says happily.

"Me either." I say honestly.

"When did you find out?" He asks.

"This afternoon right before you know?" I say smiling and he smirks.

He leans down to whisper in my ear so no one else can hear,

"Well if that's what pregnancy does to you, I am really fucking in for it aren't I?" He says huskily.

Oh yes.

9 months later...

I sit in the hospital holding our twin babies. 1 boy and 1 girl. They are absolutely beautiful and a mix of the both of us. Seth looks at me lovingly as he looks between our two miracles. "Nicholas Justin Tarantino and Charlotte Denise Tarantino." He says proudly. We named them after our parents.

"I always thought life couldn't get any better and my heart couldn't be any fuller, but I was so wrong." I tell him.

"I know. I love you so much Kendall Tarantino." He says to me.

"I love you too Seth."

I thank God every day that he brought me back to Seth. We were always meant to be. Destined from the beginning.

Milton Keynes UK
Ingram Content Group UK Ltd.
UKHW021105031224
452078UK00010B/759

9 781787 994294